MURDER STEALS THE SHOW

Rooftop Garden Cozy Mysteries, Book 7

THEA CAMBERT

Summer Prescott Books Publishing

Copyright 2020 Summer Prescott Books

All Rights Reserved. No part of this publication nor any of the information herein may be quoted from, nor reproduced, in any form, including but not limited to: printing, scanning, photocopying, or any other printed, digital, or audio formats, without prior express written consent of the copyright holder.

**This book is a work of fiction. Any similarities to persons, living or dead, places of business, or situations past or present, is completely unintentional.

CHAPTER 1

"Now don't worry about a thing. Everything will be fine."

Alice Maguire's brother, Ben, nervously wiped his glasses with the corner of his shirt, looking worriedly at his pregnant wife, Franny.

"Honey, I'm *not* worried. I *know* everything will be fine. I'm only six months along," she said in a soothing voice. "Everything's going smoothly, and I'm not going into labor for months yet."

"I know," Ben said with a little gulp. "I know." He took a deep breath. "It's just that I hate to be away while you're . . . in this condition."

"Well, you don't have to worry. I won't be alone. Alice, Owen, and I are even having a slumber party at the lake tonight!" Franny leaned against the building façade that lined one end of the rooftop garden where they all stood.

Ben gasped and pulled her away. "Don't stand there," he said. "What if the bricks gave way suddenly? You'd be down on Main Street, flat as a pancake, in seconds!"

Franny took a seat in her usual Adirondack chair in the garden, right between Alice and Owen.

"Don't worry, Ben," said Alice. "We'll take good care of Franny."

"That's right," said Owen. "We'll watch over her like two mother hens."

This seemed to appease Ben because he put his glasses back on and nodded solemnly, then went inside to gather his things.

"How are we going to deal with him for another three months?" Alice asked with a laugh, leaning back in her chair and taking a sip from her steaming mug of coffee. "Ah, Franny, that's good coffee," she said with a satisfied smile.

"It goes perfectly with my new breakfast pastry," said Owen, opening a box from his bakery, Sourdough, and setting it on the little café table. "Cream cheese puffs!"

Alice reached into the box and lifted out one of the puffs, which were made of a crisp, flaky pastry. She took a bite and closed her eyes, savoring the sweet cream cheese filling. "Owen, you've outdone yourself. And you're the best, so that's saying something!"

Owen smiled modestly. "What can I say? It's true."

The three friends had been living and working next door to each other for seven years now. Their building—one of the beautiful historic landmarks on Main Street in Blue Valley, Tennessee, was divided into three sections. Franny's coffee shop, Joe's, was on one end. Owen's bakery, Sourdough, was on the other. And Alice's bookshop, The Paper Owl, was right in the middle. Years ago, when Alice had moved into the tiny apartment above her bookshop, she'd walked out of the french doors that exited her living room, looked over the empty rooftop, and visualized a lush garden, full of climbing vines, huge pots of flowers, and plenty of the all-important twinkle lights that Alice strung wherever she went.

Once Owen and Franny moved into the apartments above their own shops, they got excited about the rooftop space, too, and between the three of them, through the years, they'd created an oasis right in the middle of Main Street—or rather, right *above* the middle of Main Street. The rooftop garden had quickly become the three friends' favorite place to meet for early morning coffee and evening glasses of wine at the end of the workday.

Their garden idea had caught on. When other shop owners up and down Main Street had seen what Alice, Owen, and Franny had done to their building, they'd been inspired to follow suit, so that now, little rooftop havens dotted the buildings up and down the street. Some merchants who lived over their businesses created their own private gardens. Some actually used the space to expand their businesses. For example, the Smiling Hound—Blue Valley's favorite pub—had added a rooftop garden that diners loved to linger in while they watched the sunset, enjoying juicy burgers and onion rings and the cool breezes blowing down from the Smoky Mountains that surrounded the little town.

Back in the fall, Franny and Alice's brother, Ben, had even gotten married in their garden. They hadn't originally planned it that way, but in the end, they couldn't have asked for a more magical place to have their special day.

Ben was the captain of the small Blue Valley police force. He was leaving town for one night, along with Alice's boyfriend of a year and a half, Detective Luke Evans. The two of them were answering a call for help from the tiny village of Runesville, which lay even farther into the mountains than Blue Valley. That was saying a lot, since Blue Valley itself was a good distance off the beaten path. It seemed that Runesville had lately experienced a rash of robberies, but without a dedicated police force, the town constable had sought the help of the nearest PD.

Ben considered the Runesville constable a good friend and was always glad to lend a hand whenever he needed one. But Franny's pregnancy had thrown him into a whirlwind of paranoia and worry. Franny couldn't hardly walk down Main Street without Ben worrying she might take a fall or be hit by a passing bicycle.

"Anyone home?" Luke Evans popped his head out of Alice's apartment, and Alice felt her heart skip happily.

"Come on out," Alice said, smiling at Luke, who came over and sat in one of the chairs.

Alice's cat, Poppy, immediately jumped into his lap, purring loudly and rubbing her whiskered cheek against his. Luke was used to this by now. Poppy was very particular about who she befriended, and Luke was aware of the honor of being chosen by the little feline. Franny poured Luke a cup of coffee.

"Thank you," he said, taking a long sip while scratching Poppy behind the ears with his free hand. "Whew. I needed that."

"Up late last night?" asked Alice.

"Yep," said Luke, yawning.

"Why? Was Finn having one of his howling dreams again?"

Luke's little black and white border collie, Finn, had

been howling in his sleep lately—which was, frankly, adorable, but also made it hard for Luke to sleep.

"No, it was your brother," said Luke with a laugh. "He called last night worried about leaving Franny."

"Oh my gosh! I had no idea!" said Franny, who must've been sound asleep when the restless Ben had called Luke to vent.

Some years ago, Ben had bought a small house on Blue Lake. When Luke had moved to town, he'd purchased the cabin just around the water's edge from Ben. Then, when Ben and Franny got married, they found they were unable to choose between Franny's cozy little apartment above the coffee shop on Main Street, and Ben's charming house on the lake. So, they chose *not* to choose and spent time in both locations. Since Blue Lake was no more than a ten-minute bike ride from Main Street, they were always close by, whether on the lake or above the coffee shop.

Tonight, Alice, Owen, and Franny looked forward to hanging out at Ben and Franny's lake house, where they'd probably pop popcorn, watch movies, and stay up way too late.

"Now remember, don't worry about a thing," Ben

said once more, bustling out of his and Franny's apartment, his Blue Valley PD duffle bag slung over his shoulder, his badge glinting in the spring sunshine. "We'll be back tomorrow evening—hopefully in time for the jousting at the faire. You call me if you need anything at all. Or, if you don't need anything, call me anyway." He bent down and kissed Franny.

"I will," Franny assured him. "You two be careful."

Luke set down his coffee cup and took Alice's hand. "Take good care of Finn for me," he said.

"I will," said Alice. "He and Poppy get to come to our slumber party tonight."

Luke laughed. "He'll love that." He kissed her hand. "See you tomorrow?" he said quietly, grinning at her.

"I'll be here," Alice said, giving his hand a squeeze.

"I can't wait to go to the faire. It's going to be amazing this year," said Ben. "Too bad Luke and I have to miss part of opening day."

The Nottingham Medieval Faire was Ben's favorite annual Blue Valley event. It came to town every spring, but this year, it was under new management, and the medieval mood would be decidedly more whimsical. Instead of just kings and knights, there would be fairies and goblins, trolls and wizards. Rumor had it there might even be a unicorn or two.

"Yes, it *will* be amazing, Benjamin," Owen said sagely. "Because Alice and I will be king and queen for the day!"

One of the new features of the Nottingham Faire was the selection of two lucky locals to serve as king and queen for the day—and because Alice had helped coordinate the event for years, she'd been chosen to act as queen. Owen, the year before, had played Robin Hood, and through a crazy twist of events, had been accused of murder. Alice suspected this was at least part of the reason he was being honored as king for a day—as recompense for the year before. Alice privately rejoiced that performing the Maypole dance was *not* on their list of duties this year. She had a long and colorful history with the Maypole dance, and she despised it.

"Don't tell Ben this," said Franny, standing and stretching after Ben and Luke had gone, "but, I don't even care about the faire. I just want those roasted turkey legs they always sell. And this year, I'm eating for two." She gave her belly a gentle pat.

Alice laughed and walked to the façade of the building to see if she could catch a glimpse of Ben and Luke leaving. "Hey. What's going on down there?" she asked, waving Franny and Owen over.

"An armored van," said Owen. "How exciting! Wonder what's inside."

"There's a police car right behind it," said Franny. "Look—they're stopping at the Heritage Museum!"

"There's Ethel," added Alice. "She looks like a busy little bee from up here."

Ethel Primrose was the keeper of local history. She was also the manager and curator for the Blue Valley Heritage Museum, half a block away—and Ethel took her work very seriously. As the three curious friends looked on, she hurried from the armored van to the police car and back again, then flitted between the van driver, who'd just lumbered out of his seat, and Officer Dewey, who'd just stepped out of his cruiser.

"It's not every day we see an armored van on Main Street in Blue Valley," said Owen, looking at Alice and Franny.

"We still have half an hour before we need to open up

shop downstairs," said Alice, reading Owen's thoughts.

"I say we amble over and see what's going on," said Owen.

"Whatever it is," said Alice, watching as Officer Dewey looked nervously up and down the street, hand resting on his belt, "Dewey seems to be breaking a sweat. Let's go."

CHAPTER 2

"May I present the fabled Scarlett Lady," Ethel Primrose said, a little breathlessly. She turned a small key in the locked box the van driver had set on the counter inside the museum, and carefully opened the lid to reveal a huge, gleaming diamond set in the middle of an elaborate arrangement of tiny red stones, cushioned on a luxurious bed of deep blue velvet.

"Whoa," Owen said under his breath.

"I've never seen anything like it," said Alice, who didn't know why she was whispering. "I mean, I've seen *pictures* of famous jewels. Like the Hope Diamond."

"The Hope Diamond is 45.52 carats," said Ethel, still

looking at the necklace in the box. "The white diamond at the center of this piece comes in at a mere twenty-three. But, when you think that the average engagement ring is one or two carats, you gain some perspective about how large this glorious stone really is."

"Is it called the Scarlet Lady because of all the red stones around it?" asked Franny.

"Yes," said Ethel. "Actually, the necklace as a whole is called the Scarlett Lady. The large diamond in the middle is known around Tennessee as the Grand Ole Gal." Ethel looked from one face to another. "You all know the legend of the Grand Ole Gal, I trust?" There was a pause. "Not even you, Alice?"

Alice, who was normally a fount of information such as this, shook her head apologetically.

"The Grand Ole Gal," Ethel said, "is a Tennessee legend. It is the nickname of a German immigrant, Elizabeth Eppinger Trantham, who lived in the seventeen and eighteen hundreds in Maury County, about three hundred miles west of here."

"What's so grand about that?" Owen said with a

snort, which earned him a stern look from Ethel and an elbow in the ribs from Alice.

"The woman was said to have lived somewhere between a hundred thirty-two and a hundred fifty-four years!" said Ethel. "She supposedly had her twelfth child at age sixty-five! How's that for grand?"

"Well, it certainly covers the 'ole' part," said Owen. He received another swift elbow from Alice.

"Where is miss, um, Elizabeth buried?" asked Alice, who loved nothing more than history and legend, and was already imagining a pilgrimage to learn more about the Grand Ole Gal.

"She's buried in an unmarked grave," said Ethel. "Anyway, the glorious white diamond in the middle has come, through the years, to be named for her. But the history of this necklace actually goes back much, much further." Ethel paused for dramatic effect. "To the sixteenth century, when Queen Isabella of Spain donated it to the explorer, Hernando de Soto—the first European explorer to set foot in our great state. He claimed the land for Spain, of course, and that's a whole other story, but that is why this necklace is connected to the history of Tennessee."

"Wow," said Alice. "Isn't it amazing that it's still intact? Seems like it would've been broken up and sold off through the centuries, doesn't it?"

"It's too exquisite a piece," said Ethel. "No one wanted to damage it. But, it's been lost, passed around, gifted, stolen . . . It was more than a hundred years from the time Spanish explorers set foot in Tennessee until the time Europeans actually started settling here. The Scarlett Lady was finally recovered in the 1800s and has been owned by several wealthy families—one of whom finally donated it to the National Museum of Natural History, which generously allows it to tour the state of Tennessee on occasion. It's a huge honor that it will spend this month right here in Blue Valley before making its way west." Ethel gave a small, proud smile. "I know someone at the museum in Washington," she added, with a wiggle of her eyebrows.

"Thanks for letting us see it," said Alice. "It's amazing."

"Gorgeous," agreed Owen.

"We'd better get to work," added Franny.

"Come back by sometime when the museum is open,"

Ethel called after them as they walked to the door. "And tell your friends and family."

When they emerged onto a still-quiet Main Street, Alice noticed Damon Huxley standing on the opposite side, leaning against a lamppost. He seemed to be watching the museum, but when he saw Alice, Owen, and Franny, he quickly pulled out his cell phone and focused on its screen.

Alice liked almost everyone she met. But, she didn't care for Damon Huxley. She seemed to be the only person in Blue Valley who hadn't taken to him when he blew into town and bought a huge house up on one of the mountains that surrounded the valley. Damon was popular almost instantly—probably a result of his good looks, charm, or wealth. Or maybe all three. But there was something about him Alice couldn't put her finger on. Something she didn't like. Maybe she wasn't nuts about the way Damon threw money around—even though that, in itself, wasn't the problem, and she was glad he was spending his dollars in Blue Valley.

It might've been the fact that Damon had made a few negative remarks about Mayor Abercrombie—and had even mentioned that he might run for mayor himself come November. It seemed presumptuous, Alice thought, to act like he knew the town and was prepared to run it after only living there for a few months.

Or, maybe it was the fact that Damon never came into the bookstore, not even for a magazine or newspaper. Alice hoped that wasn't the reason she didn't like the guy—that she was jealous that he was a regular at Joe's and even bought loaves of bread from Sourdough. *But what kind of a person didn't buy books?*

Alice kept all of these negative thoughts to herself and always greeted Damon with a smile when she happened to see him.

She did wonder, however, what he was doing out on Main Street so early that morning, and whether he was truly watching the museum or just happened to be standing across the street.

When she wondered this aloud, Owen gave a little shrug and said, "Probably saw the police and the armored van, same as us. Can't fault the guy for being curious." He turned to Franny. "I heard Damon's donating like a million dollars to make improvements at the park."

"I heard he's volunteering at toddler story time over at the library," said Franny.

Maybe that was why he never came into the bookstore! Maybe he preferred the library. It probably had nothing to do with Alice or The Paper Owl. Maybe Alice had judged him unfairly.

She smiled back in Damon's direction as she turned the sign to *Open* on the door of The Paper Owl. But Damon was too busy to notice. He was watching Taya Helms, the bartender at the Smiling Hound, walking past him, presumably on her way to the pub, where they served an amazing brunch every morning. Alice was surprised when Taya crossed to the other side of the street when she spotted Damon—seemingly in an effort to avoid him. Alice noticed Damon's eyes following Taya for a long time after she'd gone by. Then, he turned and looked right at Alice, who quickly pretended to be fiddling with the sign before going into her shop.

She let out a long sigh on the other side of the door. No, there was definitely something she didn't like about Damon Huxley. And maybe, after all, she *wasn't* the only one.

CHAPTER 3

It was a busy day at The Paper Owl, and when Alice wasn't selling books or stocking shelves, she was making last-minute phone calls, ensuring that everyone was ready for the faire to open the next day.

Owen came over from his bakery through the bookshelf door at the back of the shop. Alice loved that door. It was a childhood dream come true to have a secret bookshelf door, and even now, at the age of thirty-one, she always felt a little stealthy when she walked through it. A connecting hallway ran along the back of the building that Alice shared with Owen and Franny—and all three shops had doors that accessed the hallway, where a beautiful old wooden staircase led up to the three apartments on the second floor.

"Hello, my queen," Owen said, stepping behind the counter and immediately making himself useful by neatly tucking a customer's purchases into one of the bookstore's canvas, owl-emblazoned bags.

"What ho, your highness?" Alice answered, with a curtsy.

Owen smiled at the customer as he handed her purchase over. "Thank you for your patronage. Do come to the Nottingham Faire tomorrow, my lady," he said in his most charming British accent. "And prithee, make haste to the bakery next door, where we shall be serving fresh Welsh cakes with clotted cream and jam."

The customer giggled and gladly agreed to return the next day, then exited the shop, causing the bells above the door to jingle.

The wall that separated The Paper Owl from Joe's had a large cased opening cut into it, so that coffee shop customers could meander into the bookstore to buy the latest bestseller or today's newspaper, and bookstore customers could take their purchases, find a table, and sit and read over a cookie and a hot cup of coffee. Alice and Franny found that they got almost as many customers from within each other's shops as they did from their Main Street entrances.

"I can't wait to hear about your costumes," Franny said, propping her elbows on the counter. "How was the fitting?"

"Oh, Franny, wait until you see," said Alice. "It turns out Owen and I are king and queen—"

"Of the elves!" Owen clapped his hands gleefully. "We're *elven* monarchs! How cool is that?"

"Seriously?"

"Right down to our pointy little ears," said Alice.

"The costumes are magnificent. You have to meet the Clarks. They're the amazing new costume designers for the faire," said Owen.

"And get this: The Clarks are also acrobats. They do a show. Their names are Lois and Drake, and they're brother and sister."

Franny let out a little giggle-snort.

"What?" asked Alice.

"Oh, nothing. I was just imagining you and Ben doing

an acrobatic show," said Franny, giggling a little harder now. "Sorry! My hormones are wacky. I've generally been laughing half the time and crying the other half."

"Crying?" said Owen. "But why?"

"Don't worry. I'm not sad," Franny assured him. "Like last night, Ben and I were watching a movie, and this commercial came on where a grandmother was making this birthday cake—"

"The Fresh Flour cake mix commercial!" said Owen. "I always cry on that one, too. When the little kid gets home from school, and he's had a hard day, and none of the other kids knew it was his birthday, but then there's the grandmother, with that cake."

He and Franny both looked like they might tear up right there in the bookshop.

"Get a grip, you two," said Alice.

"Have you no heart?" Owen exclaimed.

"When can I see your elf costumes? After dinner?" asked Franny.

"Sadly, no," said Owen. "The Clarks said they needed

to make some additional alterations, so they'll deliver them in the morning."

"I thought mine already fit pretty well," said Alice, just as the bells above the door jingled and Mayor Abercrombie came in.

"There you are, Mayor Abercrombie," said Franny, turning to run back into Joe's to get a cup of French Roast with a dash of cream and a spoonful of sugar. "I was beginning to think you weren't coming in today."

"I'm running late," the mayor called after her. "But, I couldn't forgo my afternoon coffee and newspaper," he said, as Alice handed him a fresh newspaper from the rack by the counter.

The mayor usually came in around two o'clock on weekdays. He called the stop his *pick-me-up* to counteract his afternoon slump at work. He'd take a brisk walk down Main Street, saying hello to his constituents along the way, and then stop off for coffee and the latest issue of the *Blue Valley Post* before heading back over to Town Hall.

"Are we all set for the faire opening tomorrow?" asked the mayor as Franny put his cup of coffee into his hand.

"All set," said Alice, picking up her trusty clipboard with the weekend schedule on it. "You'll meet Little John and the others at the gazebo in Town Park at ten tomorrow morning for the official welcome, and then the parade out to the woods is at three."

"I love the parade," the mayor said, opening his paper and skimming the headlines.

Every year, the mayor and his staff waited on horseback as the parade progressed down Main and hooked a right onto Phlox Street. When the group passed Town Hall, King Richard, who would be played by Logan Webb this year, would greet Mayor Abercrombie, and then the whole parade would proceed out to the woods by the lake to a spot known to locals simply as *The Clearing*. It was a lovely open space surrounded by trees near the town dock at the water's edge, and it was the site of everything from weddings to concerts to the Fourth of July celebrations. That was where the evening faire festivities were held, while during the day, Main Street and Town Park were the faire hot spots.

"I'm dressing up as a wizard this year," the mayor said. "My staff are all fairies and imps and things like that. It's going to be such fun!" His smile suddenly vanished. "What's this?" he said, more to himself than to anyone else, as he looked at the newspaper.

Alice, who hadn't read today's issue yet, attempted to make out the headline upside down. "*Mayor Should Lay Off Kissing Babies and Get Down to Business.*"

"What? Who wrote that?" Owen asked, craning to see the article.

"It's a guest editorial," the mayor ground out through clenched teeth. "Written by Damon Huxley."

Alice felt the hairs on the back of her neck stand up as she remembered seeing Damon that morning, watching the museum—and then watching Taya Helms walk by in a slightly creepy way.

The mayor finished reading the editorial, his face clouded over. "The nerve of that guy!" he said, turning an angry shade of red. "Blowing into town. Acting as though he knows even the first thing about the people or the issues of Blue Valley! This is libel and I won't stand for it!" He crumpled the paper and slammed it down onto the counter. "I wish he'd never come here!"

And with that, Mayor Abercrombie took his coffee and stormed out of the bookshop.

"Wow, I've never seen the mayor so angry," said Owen, snapping up the paper and opening it back up to the editorial.

Alice and Franny leaned over his shoulders to read. After a few minutes—during which the three of them mumbled words like, *Wow*! and *Scathing*! And *Ouch*! —Owen closed the newspaper and laid it on the counter.

"Well, I can see why the mayor was so angry," he said. "That editorial was harsh."

"I don't like that Damon Huxley," said Alice.

"You don't?" Owen asked.

"He comes in for coffee a few times a week," said Franny. "Always leaves a generous tip. He seems okay to me."

"Hey, check out the front page," said Owen, pointing at the paper. "It's an article about that Scarlett Lady necklace we saw this morning."

"The Scarlett Lady," said Alice, picking up the paper.

"Oh my gosh. It says the necklace is worth twenty-five million dollars!"

"Seriously?" Owen snatched the paper from Alice's hands just as the doorbells tinkled again, and Lacie Blake and her boyfriend Zack Spears walked in.

"Lacie!" Alice said, hurrying around the counter to give the pretty young woman a hug.

Lacie was the daughter of Doug and Barb Blake, who owned the gourmet chocolate shop, Sugar Buzz, just two doors down. Lacie and Zack went to college nearby but came home often on weekends—especially when fairs and festivals were going on—to work in the bookshop and earn some extra money. Alice, who was usually at least partly in charge of those fairs and festivals, was always glad to see Lacie and trusted her to look after the shop.

"Just wanted to stop in and tell you I'll be here bright and early tomorrow morning, your highness," said Lacie, dropping a deep curtsey toward Alice.

"You heard about the queen-for-a-day thing, huh?"

"Yep. Don't worry about a thing. I can work all weekend."

"Wonderful," said Alice.

"I can't," Zack said, a note of apology in his voice. "The Nottingham Faire hired me to do set-up and tear-down. I'll be doing odd jobs for them all weekend."

"That sounds like good experience," said Alice. "I'm glad you're both home."

They caught up for a few minutes more, then Lacie and Zack headed up the street to drop in at Sugar Buzz, and Alice turned the sign to *Closed* on her door.

"We can read this later," she said, neatly folding the newspaper Owen had left on the counter and slipping it into her bag. "We don't want to be late."

CHAPTER 4

Alice locked up and the three friends walked across Main Street to the Smiling Hound, where they were meeting "Little John" Stone and his wife, Gabriella, for dinner. Since the last time the faire had come through town, Little John and Gabby, along with Logan Webb and Daniel Baker, had all become partners and now owned and managed the whole operation together. Alice, Owen, and Franny had actually had the pleasure of being present when Little John had professed his love for Gabby for the first time the year before, and six months later, they'd received a postcard announcing the happy news that the two were married.

"This year's faire is going to be amazing," Alice was saying as she pushed open the pub door.

"You got that right," a big, jovial voice said, and Alice looked up to see the smiling face of Little John, looking down at her.

"Little John! Gabby!" Alice hugged them both. "So good to see you!"

"And you all as well!" said Little John.

"How's everyone tonight?" Patrick Sullivan, owner of the Hound, said as they walked further into the pub. "I've got your table ready to go, up on the roof. Thought you'd like to eat outside, so you can catch up."

"As usual, you were exactly right," said Alice.

Everyone in Blue Valley made it into the Smiling Hound at least once a week. Whether you wanted to grab a drink or tuck into the juiciest burger in town, it was the place to be. As a result, Patrick Sullivan knew everything about everybody.

Just as the group of friends was about to head up the stairs, there was a roar of laughter from the bar area, which was just to the right of the entrance.

"Looks like Ralph's on a roll," Little John said with a laugh.

"Who's Ralph?" Franny asked.

"The guy at the end of the bar," said Gabby. "He's a riot. You'll be meeting him tomorrow at the faire. He's our jester."

"His brightly colored striped jacket kind of gave him away," said Owen. "Actually, it looks interesting paired with jeans," he added thoughtfully. "Nice to know you can dress your jester's togs down for casual evenings."

"His stage name is Wamba," said Little John.

"I see Daniel and Logan over there, too," said Alice, spotting the other two partners who owned the Nottingham Faire and giving them a wave.

"Looks like a lot of the gang is here," said Little John. "I guess everyone's settled in at the Cozy Bear."

The Nottingham Faire group usually stayed at the Cozy Bear Camp and Glamp, which conveniently lay just across the lake, so they could walk there from the clearing every evening when the festivities had ended.

Suddenly, a man whose back was turned called out, "Another round for the bar! On me!"

"Wow, someone's in a generous mood tonight," said Owen, leaning around Little John to see who it was.

When the man turned his head to the side, Alice realized it was Damon Huxley, and he looked like he was having a wonderful time, sitting smack in the middle of the faire players.

"Is that Damon?" Franny asked.

"Yes, it is," said Patrick. Alice noticed Patrick's tone was flat when he'd answered. "He's been in here every night this week, buying drinks for people, showing off." His face brightened a bit. "But, he spends a lot of money here, so I guess I can't complain."

"He doesn't have a job, does he?" Owen asked. "I wonder where his money comes from."

"I hear he's independently wealthy. Comes from a rich family," said Patrick. Then, he turned his attention to Little John and Gabby. "Hey, I'm looking forward to selling our new collection of signature ales at the faire tomorrow night," he said. "I'll be setting up the *Smiling Hound 2* over at the lake in the morning."

"Wonderful!" said Little John. "I'll be looking forward to tasting them all."

"I'll send some samples up to your table. On the house," said Patrick with a smile as the group headed up the stairs to the rooftop garden, where Taya appeared and showed them to their table.

"What are you doing up here?" Alice asked, as Taya passed out menus. "How will the bar survive without you?"

Taya laughed. "Angel's got it under control down there. Patrick's letting me wait tables up here for a while."

"Aren't the tips better down at the bar?" asked Owen.

"Honestly, I'd rather be down there. But that guy Damon Huxley is there, and I'd rather avoid him."

Alice lowered her voice and looked at Taya with concern. "Why? Is he bothering you?"

"He keeps trying to get me to go out with him," said Taya, frowning. "It's . . . it's awkward. He's basically a pompous jerk, and I wish someone would teach him a lesson. But, it probably won't be me. I figure I'll just avoid him and hopefully he'll get the message loud and clear." She cleared her throat and smiled at Little John and Gabby. "Actually, your court jester came to my rescue a while ago. He was down at the bar when Damon came in and started bugging me."

"Wamba? Oh, he's the best," said Little John.

"He's great," Taya agreed with a shy smile. "So funny and kind." Then she noticed another customer signaling that he was ready for his check, so she excused herself and promised to return to take their orders shortly.

"Seems like you've hired quite a few new folks this year," Alice said.

"We have," said Gabby. "And the faire is thriving. We've been able to share a portion of our proceeds with several worthy charities, and we've been drawing bigger crowds than ever since we changed up our management."

"One of our business tactics is hiring multi-taskers," added Little John. "Take Wamba, for instance. He's also a certified public accountant. Juggles and tells jokes by day, balances the books and handles payroll by night. Acts like a joker, but he's sharp as a tack."

"And the Clarks, who design the costumes—you met them earlier today," Gabby said, looking at Alice and Owen, "they're also acrobats and do a magic show, as well. They're absolutely brilliant!"

"Heck, our horse stunt rider is in advertising. Our bird wrangler oversees security. We've been hiring multi-talented people and it's paying off."

Taya approached the table and served a round of the Smiling Hound's signature ales to everyone except Franny, who had a chilled glass of ginger beer instead.

"I like the *Hook or Crook* best," said Owen, taking a sip of the dark brown porter. "I can taste a little chocolate in it. And vanilla, too."

"The *Hue and Cry* is my favorite," said Little John. "But I like 'em stout as possible."

"I definitely like the *Maid Marian* the most," said Alice, sipping her small glass of sweet honey mead.

After enjoying drinks, along with hearty sandwiches, burgers, and crispy fish and chips, everyone was stuffed and in need of a walk. As they exited the Hound, they noticed that the bar was quiet once more, with only the sounds of soft chatter and the clinking of glasses. Taya gave them a wave from her usual spot behind the bar.

The spring evening was perfect, with a soft breeze blowing from the vicinity of the lake, and Alice looked forward to snuggling up on the couch with a movie at Franny's. It was early yet, so the group decided to take a stroll down Main Street and do some window shopping before going their separate ways.

"I love the way Blue Valley welcomes the faire every year," Gabby said as she looked into the window of the Waxy Wick, Marge Hartfield's handmade candle shop, which was bedecked with fancy carved candles in the signature colors of the faire banners that now lined Main Street—yellow and green for Richard the Lionheart, and red and blue for his crafty brother, Prince John. One door down from there, Trinkets, Blue Valley's favorite souvenir and doodad shop, had a grouping of posters in the window touting the special, limited-edition flavors now being served at its ice cream counter.

"Ooh. *The King's Sprinkles* sounds good," said Owen. "Or *Fairy Dust Dutch Chocolate*. Yum."

"Look! The Gothic Trolls have a flavor named after them!" said Alice, pointing at the poster featuring a scoop of green ice cream with jellied chunks of something purple throughout, perched atop a chocolate-dipped cone. "Gothic Trolls Chunk . . . Hm. Not sure about that one. But the band will love it."

The Gothic Trolls were a band that played the medieval fest every spring. The rest of the year, they played at parties, weddings, and festivals, and were the favorite musical group in Blue Valley.

Just then, the blare of sirens sounded, and a police cruiser came tearing down the street from the direction of Phlox Street, where the station was located.

"What's happening?" asked Little John.

"Look! They're stopping at the museum!" Alice said, picking up her pace and hurrying down the block to where Officer Dewey had just leapt out of the car and was running into the open door of the Heritage Museum.

"Dewey, what's happening?" Alice suddenly heard a

familiar sound and turned to look across the street, but saw nothing. She grabbed Owen's sleeve. "Did you just hear . . . bells? Like jingle bells?" she asked.

"Nope," said Owen, whose full attention was on the museum. "But I think I can hear the pounding of Officer Dewey's heart. Poor guy! With Ben and Luke out of town, our little police force has dwindled significantly."

"Dewey, what's—"

Before Alice could finish her sentence, Pearl Ann Dowry came running up, screaming for help. She had her purse in one hand, and her corgi, Polly, tucked under the other arm. It was hard to tell who was more disturbed—Pearl Ann or Polly.

"I just—I think—I don't know what to do!" Pearl Ann wailed. "There was—over in the alley next to the spa! There was a prowler! I was horrified! I hit him in the head!" She held up her enormous purse. "I ran out here and saw the police car. Please come and help! He's in the alley! I think he's unconscious!"

Pearl Ann owned Blue Beauty, right next door to the museum. A scattering of trees and an alleyway ran between the two buildings. As Dewey and the whole group of onlookers walked with Pearl Ann, trying to calm her down and make sense of what had happened, she revealed that she'd just closed the spa and come out the back door into the parking lot when she saw a shadowy figure stumbling down the alleyway, babbling in a frightening, nonsensical way, and she'd hit him in the head with her purse in a valiant effort to protect herself and Polly.

Just as they approached the alley, they passed Mayor Abercrombie, hurrying down Main Street in the opposite direction, a satisfied smile on his face.

"Mayor Aber—" Alice started to call out to him as he passed, but then noticed he was busily typing something into his phone. "Strange," she said to herself. The mayor didn't usually walk by without saying hello. She glanced back as she followed the rest of the group and saw that the mayor's attention had been caught by the flashing police lights, and he had, indeed, stopped and was talking to the other officer who'd come along with Dewey.

Alice turned her attention toward the alley, which was deep in shadow, tucked as it was away from the lights that lined Main Street.

"Is he still here?" Pearl Ann asked as Alice moved forward through the crowd to have a look.

Cellphone flashlights were flipped on, and within a few seconds, a dark mass could be seen, crumpled on the ground next to the side wall of the spa.

"Who is it?" Alice heard Little John asking.

"Call an ambulance!" Gabby said.

There was a pause as Dewey, who'd been kneeling next to the body, rose to his feet. "Too late," he said quietly. "It's Damon Huxley. And he's dead."

CHAPTER 5

"So, there was a robbery . . . and now . . . there's a dead guy." Little John sat down with a heavyhearted thud on one of the benches that sat along Main Street.

"The Scarlett Lady," Alice said, shaking her head in disbelief. "It wasn't even in Blue Valley twenty-four hours, and now it's gone?"

"Gabby and I came to the museum early this afternoon," said Little John. "We didn't even know about the necklace—although we did see it. We came to see the old photos of the faire from years past." He pointed at one of the museum windows, where a grouping of photos was artfully displayed. "The display is really well done. We encouraged our whole staff to stop by and see them." He put a worried hand to his forehead.

"Alice, could you phone Ethel Primrose?" Dewey called from where he was standing, near the alley, talking to the paramedics. "Do you have her cell number? She'll want to get over here."

Alice, who did indeed have Ethel's number, dialed, her eyes settling on the worried face of Little John, who was looking at Gabby.

"It's happening again," he said quietly to his wife. "It's the curse."

Ethel answered her phone, sounding a little out of breath, and when Alice told her that the Scarlett Lady was missing, it sounded as though she dropped the phone, yelped out a quick, "Gotta go!" and then picked up the phone. The line went dead.

Five minutes later, Ethel came running down the sidewalk at top speed, tapping all the way. "I got here as fast as I could!" she said, stopping to catch her breath.

"Ethel, are those tap shoes you're wearing?" Owen asked.

"Of course they are," said Ethel. Now that she was

closer, Alice could see that she was wearing shorts, black tights, tap shoes, and a t-shirt that read *Blue Valley Tappers* across the front. "I was in the middle of my tap dance lesson down at Blue Valley Fit. Please tell me the necklace isn't gone!"

"It's not," Dewey said, coming around the corner from the alleyway. He held up the necklace, and even in the evening light, the huge diamond sparkled brilliantly.

"Oh, thank heavens!" said Ethel. "Where did you find it?"

"In the pocket of the dead man in the alley," said Dewey.

Ethel's hand flew to her heart. "Dead man? Who—"

"Damon Huxley. Looks like he stole the necklace, then died," said Dewey as the ambulance slowly pulled out of the alley and moved on down the street.

"The dead guy stole the necklace?" Little John had gotten to his feet and moved forward. "Oh, gods be praised!"

"Ms. Primrose, I'm sure you'll want to put this back in its proper place." Dewey handed over the necklace. "Let's go inside and talk about how this happened."

Ethel nodded, and began walking toward the still-open door of the museum. "Wait," she said, suddenly stopping, holding the necklace in the light. "Something's very wrong here."

"What is it?" Owen asked.

"The Grand Ole Gal is here. But all of the little rubies that surrounded it are gone!"

"Are you sure?" Dewey asked, as everyone went inside the museum to see better in the light.

"Look at it!" Ethel said, holding out the necklace so that everyone could see.

Sure enough, the Grand Ole Gal was secure, but all of the little spaces in the setting around it were completely empty.

"Get on the phone and have the paramedics check Damon's clothes. *Very carefully*," Dewey said to the other officer, who nodded and exited the building.

"Are you going to arrest me?" asked a tearful Pearl Ann, who was still holding a now-squirming Polly.

"Arrest you? Why?" asked Dewey.

"Because I'm a killer!" said Pearl Ann. "I killed Damon with my purse!"

"Oh, Pearl Ann," said Dewey, shaking his head. "No one thinks you killed him with your purse. I don't know what killed him, but the coroner, Zeb Clark, will figure that out. Meanwhile, I'm going to have you come outside and give me a full statement. Okay?"

Pearl Ann nodded, comforted that she wasn't headed for the slammer, and followed Dewey outside.

"What a tragedy," Ethel lamented, looking at the empty glass display case where the necklace had been housed. "Almost no one got to see the Scarlett Lady. And now . . . Now she's just the Grand Ole Gal."

"Isn't there an alarm system in the museum?" Alice asked.

"Yes, and apparently it worked just fine," said Owen, who'd been listening in while Dewey briefed the paramedics. "That's why Dewey came rushing down here. The alarm's wired to the front door. The police were alerted the instant it went off."

"But then the timing doesn't make sense at all," said Alice.

"I know!" said Owen. "I mean, I don't know a lot about jewelry, but surely not just anyone can dislodge, like, a hundred rubies in the few moments it would've taken Dewey to drive a block to get here from the police station. There's no way Damon would've had time to disassemble the necklace between entering and exiting the museum."

"Unless he didn't come *in* through the door," Franny said thoughtfully. "Maybe he just left that way."

"Oh, boy. I think you're right, Franny. Look," Alice said, pointing.

Everyone turned and saw the large open window on the side wall.

"Is that window wired to the alarm system?" Alice asked.

"No," said Ethel with a sad sigh. "But in our defense, it's not as if the Heritage Museum normally houses anything anyone would want to steal. In all these years, we've never had even a hint of a break-in."

That was true enough. Mostly, the museum owned

copies of old photos, blueprints of the historic buildings in town, antiques that told stories of the various phases of Blue Valley's history . . . These artifacts were valuable in their own way, but not exactly hot commodities on the black market.

"The window isn't broken," Franny observed. "Could it have been left unlocked?"

"I check all of the windows and doors every single day," said Ethel with a sniff. "It's part of my closing-up-shop checklist." Then she paused. "Except today." Ethel sat down in a nearby chair, her head in her hands. "I was running late for my tap class. How was I to know the window was unlocked? I'm sure I checked it yesterday." She groaned. "What was I thinking? How could I have been so careless?"

"So, Damon came in through the window, wisely avoiding the alarm . . . but then went out through the door, tripping the alarm?" Alice said, confused.

"Looks that way," said Owen. "But, it doesn't make sense at all. If he was going to steal the necklace, why on earth would he take the time to remove all those little stones? That's crazy."

"I guess someone else must've done that, then," said Franny, matter-of-factly.

"What do you mean?" asked Alice.

"Think about it. What if two people knew about the necklace and planned to steal it? The first person came in through the window, took the little stones, and then the second person—Damon—came in and swiped the Grand Ole Gal."

"And then ran out through the front door, setting off the alarm," Owen finished.

"Why would someone go to the trouble of taking the little stones *only*?" asked Alice. "Why not just steal the whole necklace?"

"I haven't figured that part out," said Franny.

They all sat in silence for a moment.

"You're sure that window was locked yesterday?" Alice asked, turning to Ethel.

"Positive," Ethel said with a resolute nod.

"Since the window isn't broken, someone who was in the museum today must've unlocked it."

"You might be on to something there, Alice," said Ethel, perking up a bit.

"You said only a few people got to come and see the Scarlett Lady," said Owen. "Can you remember who?"

"Yes, I can," said Ethel. "My memory is like a steel trap, but sometimes it takes me a while to recall the details." She closed her eyes and mumbled, "Now let me see . . ." Her eyes snapped open again. "Damon was here!" she said. "And then there were a few of the faire people. There were you two, of course," she said, nodding at Little John and Gabby.

"Yes, we were here," said Gabby. "But I didn't see anyone else from the faire."

"No, some others came later. Two men and a woman, I believe? And Ida Baenzinger and Jane Elkin—they're close friends of mine, and I invited them personally."

"Is that everyone?" asked Alice.

"Actually, for the Heritage Museum, that constitutes a busy day," said Ethel. "Oh—and neither Ida nor Jane could've broken in tonight."

"How can you be sure?" asked Little John.

"Because they're both in my tap class. We've all been down at Blue Valley Fit for the past hour and a half."

"And we've all been at the Smiling Hound for at least that long," said Alice, motioning at the rest of the group.

Little John let out a long sigh and looked at Gabby pointedly. Alice noticed Gabby give a tiny, worried nod.

"Ms. Primrose, could you come outside for a moment, please? We need to ask you a few questions," said Dewey from the doorway. "We're going to need you folks to clear out of here for now. This is an official crime scene."

The whole group lumbered out onto Main Street and began slowly walking back in the direction they'd come. It seemed to Alice that a year had passed since they'd window-shopped after dinner. She saw Gabby squeeze Little John's arm.

"You two seem troubled," Alice said. "Is everything okay?"

"No," Little John blurted out.

"John, my love, I'm sure you're wrong," said Gabby in a soothing voice.

"What is it? What's wrong?" Owen asked, stopping.

"This isn't the first bad thing that's happened in a town we've visited," Little John said. "I think the faire is cursed."

CHAPTER 6

After saying goodbye to Little John and Gabby, Alice, Owen, and Franny hurried back to their apartments so that Alice and Owen could grab their overnight bags, along with Poppy, before making the short trip out to the lake for their slumber party at Franny's.

Before long, they were in Franny and Ben's cozy kitchen, popping popcorn and melting butter.

"Should we watch *The Diabolical Mastermind* or *Return of the Vengeful Goblins Part Two*?" Owen called from the living room.

"We just saw a dead body, Owen," Alice answered. "Maybe something a little less spooky."

"*The Haunted Garden?*"

"Perfect."

Alice and Franny came in and plopped down on the couch with the huge bowl of buttered popcorn and Owen joined them. Luke's dog Finn and Poppy had become fast friends almost from the moment Alice and Luke had introduced them, and they came to the sofa as a team to beg for their share of the popcorn.

"I still can't get over the fact that Damon is dead," said Alice. "We just saw him this morning."

"I know," said Franny.

"It's ironic, about the necklace," said Owen, his mouth full of popcorn. "All those little red stones gone, and the big honkin' diamond safe at the museum."

"At least they saved the most valuable part," said Franny.

"It's such an unusual diamond—the Grand Ole Gal," said Alice.

"Ethel said it's one of a kind," said Franny. "And not just because it's huge. She said it's almost flawless."

"I have a theory," said Owen. "If it's really one of a kind, it'd be hard to sell, wouldn't it? I mean, everyone would know it was stolen. Those little red stones, though. They'd be easy to sell because they're not that special. You could sell them off a few at a time, maybe."

"Well, unless Damon was some kind of an eccentric jewel collector, he must've thought he could sell the Grand Ole Gal," said Alice. "Is that where his money came from, do you think? From thievery?"

"That would explain how he buys mansions and drinks for everyone but never works a day," said Owen.

The phone rang.

"It's Ben," said Franny, putting him on speaker phone.

"You okay, sweetie?" he said, his voice tense with worry. "How's the baby?"

"We're both just fine," Franny promised.

Alice and Owen added their own reassurances that Franny was safe and sound.

"We got the whole story from Dewey," Luke chimed in. "We're coming home first thing tomorrow."

"Good," said Alice.

Finn, hearing the voice of his master, gave a little enthusiastic bark.

"Hey, Finn. Good boy," said Luke.

"Poor Pearl Ann," said Alice.

"Yeah. She thinks she killed Damon with her purse," said Owen.

"From what Zeb says, it wasn't Pearl Ann that killed him," said Ben.

"Really? What did kill him?" asked Alice.

"Now you know I'm not going to give you any details while the investigation is open," said Ben. "Let's just say that Dewey had ingested something that didn't go well with the copious amounts of alcohol he'd apparently been drinking."

"We could've guessed the part about the alcohol," said Owen. "We saw him having a high old time at the Hound."

"You mean, like he ingested a drug?" asked Alice.

Ben sighed. "Yes, like a drug," he said. Then, changing the subject, he told Franny how much he was looking forward to going with her to the faire the next day and elicited promises from Owen and Alice that they would watch Franny like two protective hawks.

They hung up and snuggled in for their movie. Franny began crying during the scene where the old gardener got locked out of the garden, so they hit pause while she ran to get a box of tissues.

"No one cries during *The Haunted Garden*!" Alice called after her. Then she turned to Owen. "Did you hear what Little John said about the faire being cursed?" she asked, getting up from the couch and digging her tablet computer out of her bag.

"Well, we all know Little John can be a little on the dramatic side sometimes," said Owen.

"Get your phone," Alice said, and when Franny came back with the tissues, she added, "Franny, you get your phone, too. I've got the faire's website open." She scrolled through the pages until she found what she was looking for. "Here it is. A list of all the places the faire has visited so far this year, along with the dates they were in those places. Looks like they've been working their way east from Nashville since January. They were in Hendersonville January third through sixth." Alice turned to Owen. "Check the police records in the local newspaper around that time span."

Owen nodded, and began typing into his phone.

"Franny, you check Smithville on January eighth through the eleventh."

One by one, they ticked off the towns the faire had stopped in. And one by one, they checked the local police reports in those towns.

"Little John was right," Alice finally said. "There have been bad things happening in every single town they've stopped in. The common denominator seems to be theft. Mostly art and jewelry."

"As far as I can tell, no arrests have been made in any of these cases," said Owen.

"So, it's not that the faire is cursed," said Franny. "It's just that they've got a thief in their midst."

"Seems like it," said Alice with a sigh. "And maybe a murderer as well."

CHAPTER 7

The lake was magical in the early morning. The sun rose on Ben and Luke's end of the lake in the east, and set in the west, down by the Cozy Bear Camp and Glamp, so a golden light filtered through the trees behind Alice, Owen, and Franny as they sat on the dock, watching a thin layer of steam fog roll along the water's surface and dissipate into the air.

"We should have our morning coffee out here on the water all spring," said Owen, taking a sip from his mug. "Oh!" He hopped up and jogged back into the house, returning moments later with a plate of his signature sin-amon rolls. "I warmed these up in the oven. Thought we should carb load before our big day." He gave Alice a wink.

"Queens do not carb load," said Alice, peeling off the doughy outer strip of her roll and savoring the spices and vanilla cream cheese frosting. "We nibble."

"Well, next week, after your reigns have come to an end, we need to do a little extra jogging," said Franny.

Once they were all dressed and ready to go, they hopped into Owen's SUV. They'd driven over to Franny's the night before instead of riding their bikes since they'd brought Poppy over. Poppy loved riding in the car but would not abide a bicycle basket.

"Slow down," Alice said, as they approached the clearing by the lake where various members of the faire's staff were busy setting up for the evening festivities. "There are the Clarks. Let's ask them about our costumes."

They stopped to admire the jousting ring, with its colorful flags flapping in the cool morning breeze. The bird show area was already marked off and benches were set out in rows around the stage. They waved at Patrick Sullivan, who was off in the trees, setting up his outdoor tavern, the Smiling Hound 2, with little tables and chairs scattered around it.

"Good morning!" Alice said, as they approached Lois and Drake Clark.

"Good morning!" said Lois, standing up straight and stretching her back.

"What's this you're working on?" asked Owen.

"This is the arrow-shooting booth. People can stop by and try their luck."

Owen let out a little groan. "I know all about that booth. It's the one thing I'm not planning to do at the faire this year."

Drake laughed. "We heard about last year," he said, referring to the year before, when Owen had been the faire's Robin Hood. Ironically, Owen had proven to be a terrible shot.

"This is our friend Franny," Alice said, linking arms with Franny.

"Very nice to meet you, Franny," said Drake, doffing his hat and bowing cordially.

"Congratulations are in order," Lois said, nodding at Franny's round belly. "How wonderful." She looked at her brother. "I'd love to design a costume for a *lady-in-waiting*, as it were."

"From what I hear, you're brilliant and the costumes are gorgeous," said Franny.

"We're very proud to be part of the Nottingham Faire," Lois said graciously.

"You look pretty busy," said Alice. "Would it be more convenient for you if Owen and I picked up our costumes, so you don't have to drop them by the shop?"

"Oh, it's no inconvenience," said Drake. "We're headed over to the campground after we finish up here. We've got the costumes in our . . . it's really not a tent. It's more of a very comfortable . . ."

"Yurt," said Lois. "We're glamping. It's wonderful! Plenty of space. A beautiful view of the water. It's so nice that we can walk right around the lake to get here. This really is a wonderful town. It's my favorite so far."

Alice loved hearing Blue Valley complimented. "We're glad you're here," she said. She spotted Lacie's boyfriend, Zack, across the clearing. He gave a little wave. "We'll see you later then," said Alice, giving the Clarks a smile, and she, Owen, and Franny walked across the clearing to say hello to Zack.

"Working hard or hardly working?" said Owen as they approached Zack.

Zack laughed. "The faire people have been really nice to me," he said. "I'm learning a lot." He glanced around. "Did you hear about the dead guy over by the museum? That Damon Huxley guy?" he asked in a low voice.

"We were actually at the scene," Alice said. "Awful."

"Lacie and I have been off at school, so we hadn't really met him, but I hear he stole that diamond necklace Ethel Primrose had on display."

"Yep—or part of it, anyway," said Owen.

Zack frowned in confusion.

"Hey, Zack," said Alice, keeping her voice down. "You've met a lot of the faire staff. Is anyone acting suspicious?"

"Suspicious?"

"Strange? Nervous? Odd?"

"You've just described Wamba," said Zack with a chuckle.

"Wamba? The jester?"

"Yep. He's right over there." Zack pointed to an area next to the jousting ring, where Wamba was up on a wobbly ladder, hanging a banner.

"Thanks, Zack," said Alice. "We'll see you later."

When they walked up to the jousting ring, Alice saw the ladder start to tip. Owen ran forward and grabbed it, then held it steady.

"Oh. Thank you," said Wamba. "But you needn't worry. I've fallen many a time. Always land on my feet." He smiled cheerfully, then came down the ladder, jumping to the ground once he'd reached the fourth-to-the-bottom rung. "You three look familiar. Where have I seen you before?"

"We're the king and queen of the elves," Owen said.

"We crossed paths with you briefly last night, at the Smiling Hound," said Franny.

"Ah! Of course!" Wamba bowed low to Franny, then

turned to Alice and Owen. "Your highnesses, I am honored to be your court jester today."

"We're the ones who are honored," said Alice. "We've never had a jester before."

"Speak for yourself," said Owen.

"I insist that it is I who bears the honor today, my lady," said Wamba, perfectly in character. "But fear not—I shall not burden you in any way. My lot are invisible until we are needed. That is the mark of a good jester. Rest assured, I will be near, if you need me."

Alice noticed something over her shoulder had caught Wamba's eye, and his face had darkened a bit, the silly smile slightly fading. She looked in the direction of his gaze, but saw only the rest of the faire staff, working around the clearing.

"Is everything okay, Wamba?" she asked.

His eyes snapped back to Alice. "But of course! What could possibly be amiss?"

Alice took a step closer to Wamba, making the decision to pry a little while she had the chance. "Perhaps you were upset by the news of a death in our fair city," she whispered.

At that, Wamba's face changed, and he suddenly looked more like an accountant than a jester. "I did hear about that," he said, clearing his throat. "Sad news. I hope the man was not a close friend to any of you."

When they shook their heads, Wamba took back on his character. "But 'tis true, is it not, that when people *get* in the way, they sometimes *pass* away? Before their time, indeed." He made a sad face. "We might all be warned by this cautionary tale."

"Except that it's no tale," Owen said slowly. "We saw the dead man. We also saw the gaping holes left in a very valuable diamond necklace."

"A cutpurse or a killer? Among *us*, do you think?" asked Wamba, fanning his arm across the clearing.

"The police will find the culprit," said Franny.

"But until they do," Alice added, "we're keeping our eyes open."

Wamba looked at the ground. "Well, I suspect," he said in a non-theatrical voice, "that if you find the killer, you'll find the missing jewels. And if you find the jewels, you'll find the killer."

Alice's eyes widened at this. "Wamba, is there something you'd like to tell us? Or the police?"

Wamba looked around nervously and shook his head. "No, my lady. But, you have my word, if I knew anything beyond a shadow of doubt, I would waste no time in telling the authorities."

Alice stepped back a bit. "Good," she said with a nod.

Just then, Logan and Daniel walked up. After greeting Alice, Owen, and Franny, they told Wamba it was time to rehearse the scene when King Richard would face Prince John that afternoon on Main Street before the parade.

Wamba offered another low bow. "Until later then, my lieges," he said, his smile not quite reaching his eyes.

CHAPTER 8

"Are my ears on straight?" Owen asked, turning to Alice.

"Yep. Are mine?"

"Perfectly." Owen smiled at Alice's outfit—from the simple silver diadem that fit around her head, coming to a V on her forehead, to the full-length dusky rose gown, which appeared to be made of layer upon layer of gossamer fabric in various earthy tones, scattered with tiny shimmering sparkles in complimentary colors, with sleeves that looked like leafy lace, fitted perfectly to Alice's arms. Alice's red curls were left loose under her crown and hung down around her shoulders.

Owen, on the other hand, was wearing a striking wig. His pointy ears stuck out through his long platinum hair, which cascaded down his back, the strands around his face strategically plaited to keep it from blowing into his eyes. Over this he wore a crown similar to Alice's, and a long, shimmering robe and cape combination rounded out the ensemble.

"You look very . . . *Lord of the Rings*-y," said Alice.

"High praise, indeed," said Owen with a satisfied smile.

The Clarks had brought the costumes over to The Paper Owl around lunchtime, and true to her word, Lois had even whipped up a little something for Franny—a lovely empire waisted confection in a cornflower blue exactly the color of Franny's eyes, studded with tiny white jewels all over the bodice.

By two-thirty that afternoon, as they'd been instructed, Alice and Owen were waiting for their cue to go onstage. They were hidden behind a curtain next to the stage that had been constructed smack in the middle of Main Street. A large crowd had gathered for the official opening ceremony of the faire where, as he did every year, King Richard the Lionheart would approach on horseback from one end of the street, as though returning from the Crusades, and Prince John would approach from the other. The two would have it out on the stage, until John would challenge Richard to a joust. Then, the whole company would set out for the clearing in the woods, led this year by the newly crowned elven nobility. Onlookers would join the parade, on horseback, bike, or foot, and follow along.

Franny would be watching the ceremony from the audience. She would drive out to the lake in Owen's SUV and meet up with the group at the clearing, since a concerned Ben had strongly urged her not to ride a horse while pregnant.

"Everyone ready back here?" asked Little John, poking his head through the curtains.

Alice heard the crowd cheering wildly, and when Little John moved the curtains aside, she could see Wamba on stage, doing an impressive juggling act.

"Wow. Are those really on fire?" Owen asked.

"Oh yeah," said Little John, glancing over his shoulder. "Wamba juggles all kinds of things. Flaming torches. Daggers. Swords."

"Numbers," Owen added with a snicker. When Alice rolled her eyes at him, he said, "What? Who doesn't love a little accounting humor?"

"King Richard and Prince John are about to come this way," said Little John. "They'll argue onstage, then pronounce that you are to be king and queen of the faire. Then, you'll mount your horses, which Gabby and I will have waiting for you right next to the stage, and we'll be off. Sound good?"

"Yep," said Alice with a flutter of butterflies in her stomach at the thought of standing before the crowd. She wished Luke was there.

"We got this," said Owen, giving Little John a thumbs-up, which Little John returned before closing the curtain and going back to the stage, where he and Robin Hood, along with a group of Merry Men, boisterously cheered King Richard on.

Owen stuck his head out of the curtain to take a peek.

"Owen! Get back in here!" hissed Alice.

"Oh, look! It's Officer Dewey!" said Owen, and before Alice could stop him, he'd waved Dewey over to the curtain and yanked him inside with them.

"Who—oh, wow!" Dewey's brown eyes widened. "You both look so magical!"

"Thanks," Owen said. "How's your investigation going?"

Dewey peered out the slightly open curtain at Wamba, who had just jumped onto Prince John's back and was pretending to whack him in the head with a scepter of some kind while the audience hooted with laughter and applause. "Jesters are the best." Dewey sounded a little regretful when he said this.

"But?" Owen prodded.

Dewey looked back at Alice and Owen. "I hope the jester isn't a criminal," he finally said.

"Wamba? Why would you suspect him?" asked Alice.

"Pearl Ann will tell you this herself—she's already told half the town, I imagine. When Damon was in the alley, before Pearl Ann hit him with her purse, he was ranting about a jester."

"Well, that's both odd and bizarre," said Owen, frowning.

"And, of course, we've already questioned Wamba."

Dewey pointed a thumb over his shoulder toward the stage. "At this point, there's no proof he was at the scene. No proof of anything. He seems like a good guy." Dewey shook his head. "I wish Ben and Luke were here."

"Dewey, you are perfectly capable of solving this on your own," said Owen in his patented pep-talk voice. "And we're going to help you."

Dewey smiled and nodded, then frowned in confusion when the second part of Owen's encouraging remark sunk in.

"Now buck up. It's going to be okay." Owen patted Dewey on the back.

Outside, the crowd cheered for King Richard, who was now on stage, sparring verbally with Prince John.

"Is there any sign of the little red stones that were missing from the Scarlet Lady?" Alice asked hurriedly, knowing they were almost out of time.

"No. They weren't on Damon's body anywhere. They're still missing."

"I accept your challenge!" King Richard said from the stage. "But before we go to battle, I am privileged to introduce a king and queen of noble blood, visiting us today from a far-off land! They shall preside over our joust!"

Alice heard Franny whooping and whistling before she and Owen had even made it out onto the stage, and somehow, her nerves were calm. Everyone cheered, and after waving, bowing, curtsying, and blowing kisses, Alice and Owen were escorted to their horses at the side of the stage.

"You're eating this up," Alice said to Owen through her smile.

"Can I help it if the people love me?" said Owen, waving once more before climbing onto his silvery steed.

The whole cast of the show paraded down Main Street, with festival-goers filing in behind them for the short walk to the lake.

"You two stole the show!"

Alice turned to see Lois, dressed as a fairy, riding next to her brother just behind them.

"That's because of our costumes," said Alice with a

smile. "They really are exquisite. I feel like a real queen in this gown!"

"That makes me so happy!" said Lois.

"You two made the whole process fun," said Drake, catching up. "We love meeting new people in each town we visit, and one of our favorite challenges is touching up the costumes to suit our subjects."

"Well, you did a beautiful job," said Alice. "I promise I'll be careful not to spill anything on this gown. The fabric is so delicate. And all of the little jewels!"

Lois laughed. "Too bad they're not real, like the diamonds that were stolen from the museum. We were so sorry to hear about that. But just imagine, in the old days, queens really had gowns bejeweled with precious stones. They'd be worth a fortune!"

"It's so odd, isn't it, that only the smaller stones from that necklace are missing?" Alice mused. "I mean, why would someone leave the giant stone behind?"

"Red diamonds are extremely rare," said Drake. "Even very small ones."

"Did you get a chance to see the necklace before it was damaged?"

"Sadly, no," said Lois. "But we read all about it in the paper."

Alice nodded, remembering the front-page article from the day before, which she still hadn't gotten around to reading.

"Tally ho and away we go!" Wamba came riding up on his smaller horse and steered in between Alice and Owen.

The Clarks waved and fell back as the whole group turned onto Phlox Street and approached Town Hall, where the mayor and his staff waited.

"Your personal court jester is here!" Wamba's striped jacket jingled as he reached into a large pocket in his silken pants and pulled out a scepter with a jester's head on top.

"Oh, look," said Owen. "You have a little friend with you today."

"I bring him along for laughs!" Wamba made it seem like the little jester head was the one doing the talking instead of him.

Alice suddenly realized why the jingling bells attached to the hemline of Wamba's jacket sounded familiar. She'd heard bells just like them the night before, in the darkness at the museum.

Wamba chuckled at Alice's expression, which had turned serious. "Fear not, my lady," he said, shaking the scepter at her. "Tis only a fool's bauble."

Alice shook off her suspicion. "You even have matching hats," she observed, pointing at the jester's hats both Wamba and his scepter wore—adorned with bells and tiny jewels like the ones on Alice's gown.

"But of course," said Wamba. "We are twins."

"Except I have all the brains!" Wamba made the scepter say. He pulled out a pocket watch and popped it open. "I've got to run," he said.

"Beautiful watch," said Alice, admiring the intricate scrolling on the silver case.

"Thanks," said Wamba, popping the watch back into his pocket. "It's an antique. I collect them." Then, with a quick, "See you at the joust, your highnesses," he trotted away to greet the mayor.

Alice quickly pulled out her cell phone, which she'd tucked into the little jeweled bag she carried.

"Alice! Elves do not have cell phones. Put that away!" Owen scolded.

"After I text Dewey," Alice said, tapping a message into her phone.

"What's going on?"

"Did you hear Wamba's bells jingling?"

"Well, yes . . ."

"Those were the same bells I heard last night. Remember?"

"No."

"When I asked you if you heard bells? Right before we found the dead body?"

"Oh, yeah. So, you think they were the same bells? Wamba's bells?"

"He was wearing that same striped jacket when we saw him at the Smiling Hound, in the bar. The jacket with the bells on it."

"Poor Dewey's going to be so depressed. He loves jesters."

Just as Alice finished messaging Dewey, she received a text from Luke.

"Oh, no!" she moaned.

"What?"

"Now I know why Luke and Ben are running late. There's been a landslide up in the mountains. Luke says they're stuck, and it looks like they won't get home until tomorrow."

"That means another slumber party night!" said Owen.

By this time, the formal greetings between Mayor Abercrombie, as 'ruler' of Blue Valley, and King Richard had taken place, and the mayor, in full-blown wizard regalia, had joined the parade along with much of the staff at Town Hall.

Jake Shannon, the mayor's assistant, trotted over to Alice and Owen.

"Nice costume, Jake," said Alice.

"Yeah. What are you supposed to be?" asked Owen.

"I'm a troll. Can't you tell?"

"Of course we can tell," said Alice quickly, even though she *hadn't* been able to tell. "You have that green robe and those big . . . ears. And that necklace made out of—are those bones?"

"Yes. Well, they're supposed to be teeth," said Jake, looking down at his necklace.

"Teeth?" Owen asked, repulsed. "I thought trolls were those cute, stubby creatures with the fluffy, brightly colored, cotton-candy hair."

Jake didn't seem amused by this description. "Owen, I'm a *real* troll," he said. "Not some cartoon troll."

"What's up?" asked Alice, changing the subject as she sensed that Jake had something more serious on his mind than troll costumes.

"I need to talk to Ben and Luke. Are they back from Runesville yet?"

"No, and it doesn't look like they'll be back until tomorrow now," said Alice. "But you could call them," she suggested.

Jake frowned. "I'd really like to talk to them in person."

"Jake, you look troubled," said Owen. "What's wrong?"

"It's . . . it's about what happened last night at the museum. I need to show them something."

"Well, Dewey's here somewhere. He'll probably be out at the clearing. You could show him," suggested Alice.

Jake didn't reply for a while. "Luke and Ben will be back tomorrow?" he finally asked.

"Yes, that's what Luke said," Alice assured him.

"Okay. Thanks." Jake trotted back to the mayor's side.

"Wonder what's going on with him?" Alice said.

"Who knows. But we're falling behind," said Owen. "We're supposed to be up at the front of this parade. Shake a leg, your highness."

CHAPTER 9

They arrived at the clearing to find it transformed, with twinkling lights strung in all the trees, and booths and displays scattered here and there—and most impressive of all, the jousting ring, with its flags flying, ready for a night of entertainment.

Alice and Owen were escorted to the Royal Box to watch King Richard and Prince John face off. They'd invited Franny to join them as their special guest, and thankfully, Owen had bought a giant bag of kettle corn from Kernel Pop's popcorn cart on the way in. Meanwhile, Franny was already halfway through her second roasted turkey leg by the time the show began.

When King Richard rode his horse up to the box,

Alice bestowed her handkerchief upon his lance, and Owen stood to read the joust-opening lines from the script that was waiting for him at his throne.

Once the joust was underway, Alice slipped her phone out of her bag and sent a double text to Ben and Luke, asking if Jake Shannon had happened to get in touch with them. Ben quickly answered that he had not.

"I wonder what was bothering Jake," Alice said, looking at Owen.

"What are you talking about?" asked Franny.

Alice and Owen filled Franny in on how strangely Jake had acted during the parade.

"I wonder if it has anything to do with the mayor being at the scene of the crime last night," said Franny.

"And smiling like the cat that got the canary," added Owen.

Alice sighed. "Surely the mayor had nothing to do with Damon Huxley's death," she said.

"Surely not," said Owen. "But he did hate the guy."

"Such serious faces for such a jolly time!" Wamba appeared as if from nowhere at the entrance to the box. "How do my highnesses find the entertainment?"

"We're enjoying it immensely," Owen said. "We elves love a good joust."

"Good, good," said Wamba. "May I ask your royal permission to bring my own guest into the box?" He motioned toward the two empty chairs at Alice's side.

"Of course, you may bring a guest," said Alice. "Who is it?"

"My own lady," Wamba said, a light flush coming to his cheeks. "The most beautiful person in this kingdom or any—excepting yourself, of course, your highness."

"Thank you," said Owen.

"I think he meant me," said Alice. "Thank you, Wamba. Bring your lady friend."

Wamba did a little dance, then disappeared, and returned a moment later with his lady—who turned out to be Taya, from the Smiling Hound.

Taya, dressed in dazzling emerald green, greeted everyone and took the seat next to Alice.

"This is the best view in the house!" she said, looking down at the king and prince, who had now leapt off their steeds and battled it out with the sword. She smiled at Wamba. "Thank you, Ralph—I mean, Wamba—for thinking of me. This is wonderful."

"It is my great pleasure," said Wamba with a humble nod.

"I think he really likes her," Owen whispered to Alice. "He keeps blushing just like you do whenever Luke's around."

Alice elbowed Owen, and then clapped as King Richard won the fight and waved to the royal onlookers, and then to the roaring crowd.

Wamba jumped up. "I must go down and perform for a moment," he said. "Please, watch over my lady until I return."

Alice, Owen, and Franny all nodded, and Wamba literally jumped over the front of the box and landed feet-first on the ground below.

"Wow, that guy is . . ." Owen peered over the railing.

"Agile," Alice finished. As Wamba regaled the crowd with a combination of joke-telling and juggling various objects, Alice turned to Taya. "Looks like you've made a new friend, Taya," she said.

"He's so kind. So chivalrous," said Taya, smiling down at Wamba, who glanced up at the box every now and then.

"So protective?" asked Alice. Even from on high, she could hear the bells on Wamba's jacket jingling—a constant reminder of the bells she'd heard the previous night.

The smile left Taya's face. "You three seem to be as good at crime-solving as the police," she said tentatively. "Maybe even better."

There was a pause as they waited for her to continue.

"Do you happen to know what killed Damon?" Taya finally said.

Alice knew it wasn't exactly common knowledge, but she also knew that in light of Taya's apparent close relationship with Wamba, Taya's reaction to the truth might be telling, and they needed all the clues they could get.

"They haven't gotten the details yet," Alice said. "But, it looks like he ingested something. Or had a bad reaction to something. Like a drug."

"Which is great news for Pearl Ann," Owen added, leaning over. "Because she and her giant handbag are now off the hook."

"Ingested something?" Every drop of color drained from Taya's face.

"Taya?" Alice put a hand on Taya's arm.

"I am returned, my lady!" Wamba had somehow climbed the front of the box and in one swift movement, had swung himself over the railing.

"Man, this guy is strong!" said Owen. "What are you? Some kind of gymnast?"

But Wamba didn't seem to hear. He was looking at Taya, his eyes full of concern. "Come, my lady," he said quietly. "The joust is over. Let us walk a little." With that, he took her hand and escorted her out of the box.

"Well, that was strange," said Franny, wiping her fingers on a napkin after polishing off the turkey drumstick and half the bag of kettle corn.

"He's protecting her, don't you think?" asked Alice.

"But from what, exactly?" asked Owen.

"I heard those bells just after Damon was killed," said Alice. "What if Wamba killed Damon to protect Taya?"

"It's also true that Taya herself had good reason to dislike Damon," said Owen thoughtfully.

"As did the mayor," said Franny.

"So, there are three suspects," said Alice. "Taya, who just had a very strong reaction to the news that Damon died by ingesting some kind of drug. The mayor, who we just yesterday heard saying that he wished Damon had never come to Blue Valley. And Wamba, who obviously cares for Taya and might've been protecting her from Damon."

"And, we *know* the mayor was at the scene of the crime because we saw him," said Franny.

"We're pretty darn sure Wamba was there, too, because I heard his noisy jacket," said Alice.

"We'll talk about this later," said Owen, getting up. "We have to go now."

"What are your royal duties for the rest of the night?" asked Franny, wobbling a little as she stood.

"We have to walk amongst our people," said Owen. "You know—photo ops, waving, being graciously fabulous."

"After that, we're done, and are no longer king and queen of anything," said Alice.

"Speak for yourself," said Owen. "You know, I have a hankering for some of that *Hook or Crook* ale of Patrick's."

"Good idea," said Alice. "We can bring up Damon. See if he knows anything. To the Smiling Hound 2!"

After much waving and having their photos taken with faire-goers, Alice, Owen, and Franny finally made it to Patrick Sullivan's makeshift tavern in the trees. There were lights strung all around the miniature Smiling Hound, and tables scattered about the area, where patrons sat enjoying drinks and plates laden with medieval-themed snacks, such as cheeses, stuffed eggs, tiny meatballs, and fry bread made over the fire that Patrick and his crew were carefully watching. As royalty, Alice and Owen earned a free drink, and Patrick threw in a ginger beer for Franny to wash down her third turkey leg of the night, which she'd managed to procure as they'd walked past Friar Tuck's Turkey on their way to the Hound.

As it turned out, they weren't even the ones to broach the subject of the case. Patrick beat them to it.

"Any leads on the robbery or murder—because I *know* you three are investigating," he said with a wink.

"Well," Alice said, a twinkle in her eye, "we *would* like to get your thoughts on Damon Huxley."

"My thoughts? Why?"

"Because you're a good judge of character," Owen quickly said. "You know everyone in town, you constantly observe people . . ."

"We're just trying to figure out why someone might want Damon dead," added Franny.

"Want him dead? I was under the impression that the

thing was a botched robbery of some kind," said Patrick. "If you want my impression of Damon, it wasn't good, to be honest. I never did like him."

"Neither did I," Alice admitted. "But, I couldn't put my finger on why."

"Neither could I!" said Patrick. "Just had a bad feeling about the guy. So did Taya."

"Did she?" asked Owen, pretending not to already know as much.

"You know, Taya always sees the best in people," said Patrick. "But she didn't like Damon. I even let her wait tables upstairs when he'd come into the bar. He made her very uncomfortable."

"He kept hitting on her, I think," said Alice. "He wasn't too good at taking no for an answer."

"Well, that Taya is the big-hearted sort," said Patrick, smiling at a customer who had just approached and was looking over the menu. "She must've forgiven the guy before he left the Hound last night."

"Why do you say that?" asked Alice.

The customer stepped forward and asked for a Golden

Dragon, which Patrick quickly served, thanking the customer kindly. Then he turned back to Alice, Owen, and Franny.

"Because she said she'd go back to work the bar last night before Damon and the rest of them left," he said. "She even made him a complimentary drink."

CHAPTER 10

"I think my feet are starting to swell." Franny leaned over her own belly to look at her sparkling slippers.

"We should get you home," said Alice, checking the time on her phone. "It's only seven-thirty, but it's been a long, busy day."

"The faire goes on until midnight," said Franny. "Are you sure you don't want to stay longer?"

"It'll be way more fun at your house," said Owen. "We can check on Poppy and Finn, and then go sit out on the dock and enjoy this beautiful spring evening."

"That sounds like heaven," said Franny, breathing a sigh of relief.

As the three friends began the short walk from the clearing to Ben and Franny's lake house, Alice spotted Jake Shannon, walking through the trees as though he was headed home, as well. Alice told Owen and Franny to hold up a second, and she jogged over to Jake.

"Where's your horse?" she called.

"What? Oh, hi, Alice," Jake said. "The wranglers came and transported the horses back out to the farm. I'm headed home to my family." He jingled his keys and nodded toward the parking area, where he'd apparently left his car earlier in the day.

"Didn't Holly and the kids come to the faire?"

"Oh, yes," he said with a smile. "They had a great time. But you know how it is with little ones. Holly took them home to get them ready for bed."

"Did you, um, decide to call Ben and Luke, by the way? Or talk to Dewey? About whatever was worrying you?" Alice couldn't think of a subtle way to ask, so she just came out with it.

"No," Jake said, looking worried. "But they're coming home tomorrow, right?"

By this time, Owen and Franny had walked over and joined them.

"They should be," said Franny.

Alice took a step closer to Jake. "Jake, something has clearly upset you. Is there anything we can do to help?"

Jake looked from Alice, to Owen, to Franny, and finally sighed and said, "I'd like to show you something."

Everyone automatically stepped closer still, as Jake scrolled through photos on his phone, finally stopping at one and pausing before showing the others.

"What—*who*—is that?" Owen said, frowning.

"It looks familiar." Franny squinted at the photo.

"That's because we just saw it last night," said Alice, looking back up at Jake. "That's Damon Huxley. After he was killed."

"And obviously before the police and ambulance came," said Owen, his eyes widening at the realization of what they were seeing.

"That's correct," said Jake. "Mayor Abercrombie took this photo."

"Sick!" said Owen, then quickly cleared his throat and added, "I mean, what an odd choice of subjects for a photo."

"Doesn't bode well, does it." Jake said this more as a statement than a question.

"We saw the mayor there last night," Alice said. "He looked . . . sort of . . . smug?"

"He *felt* sort of smug," Jake admitted. "He'd just taken a picture of what he *thought* was a drunk, passed-out Damon Huxley."

"Why would he do that?" asked Franny.

"Did you read yesterday's paper?" asked Jake.

"That editorial Damon wrote? Yep," said Alice.

"We didn't believe a word of it," said Owen.

"The mayor was pretty upset by that article—and even more upset that Damon said he was going to make a run for mayor next fall," said Jake.

"We know he was upset. We were there when he read the paper," said Owen.

"When he was walking home from Town Hall last night, he saw Damon and snapped a photo, then sent it straight to me. He thought there might be a time when the people of Blue Valley would need to be shown who they were voting for. He even thought it might be a good idea to leak the photo to Jane at the *Blue Valley Post*." Jake let out a long sigh. "It's not the way we conduct ourselves at Town Hall, normally. But the mayor was feeling threatened, and a little desperate, and now, well, this looks pretty bad. I mean, let's face it. He did have motive to get rid of Damon, and the fact that he took a picture of the guy after he was dead, well, that doesn't look good."

"Why don't you just delete the photo?" asked Owen.

"Because I don't want to cover something up or hide something I shouldn't. It doesn't feel right. Add to that the fact that Mayor Abercrombie copied both Jane *and* me on this photo—"

"And you're up a creek," said Owen. "So, the *Post* has the photo and knows who took it?"

"Yep," said Jake, nodding slowly. "I called Jane and

asked her not to run it. Told her what had happened. But, she hasn't made her final decision on that yet. This is a hot news item now. I just . . . I don't know Officer Dewey that well, but Luke and Ben are personal friends, and I want to ask them what to do about this." He paused. "You know what would be even better?"

"What?" asked Alice.

"If you three could solve this thing first. Before the guys even get home."

"Well, we're—"

"I know it's a lot to ask, but the mayor's reputation has taken a few hits lately, thanks to Damon. With this photo and the fact that it's common knowledge the mayor had a score to settle with him . . . Look, the job and this town mean everything to Mayor Abercrombie. If I can possibly protect him, I'd like to. Please, if you have any idea who killed Damon Huxley, prove it."

"We'll try," Alice said, Owen and Franny nodding their agreement.

"Thank you," Jake said, and walked on toward

his car.

❦

"Wow, it feels good to get out of that costume!" Alice said, coming into Franny's cozy living room wearing her comfiest sweats.

"I'll be glad to give my gown back to the Clarks in the morning," said Franny, who had changed into her favorite mommy-to-be elastic-waisted pants and a t-shirt. "I was so afraid I'd trip over something and tear it or get it dirty, as off balance as I'm starting to be with this belly." She smiled and patted her tummy.

"I'm going to miss being the elf king," said Owen mournfully. "Tomorrow when we go to the faire, we'll just be normal people again."

"Oh, I don't think there's much danger of that," said Alice with a laugh.

They took a little time to play with Finn and Poppy, and then made their way down the gentle slope of Franny and Ben's yard to the dock, where they took seats in comfortable chairs and watched the last embers of a beautiful sunset on the far side of the lake.

"It's so peaceful here," said Alice. "How do you like living on the lake?"

"Don't get me wrong. I love our apartment over the coffee shop," said Franny. "But this place is magical. We take evening walks along Lake Trail. We sit on the dock with our feet in the water on warm days. It's going to be a wonderful place for a child to grow up."

"What's that they say about a red sky at night?" asked Owen, marveling at the pink-tinged water. "*Red sky at night, you're in for a fright?*"

"Uh, no," said Alice. "Red skies at night are supposed to mean peaceful sailing, I think."

Alice's cell phone beeped.

"Maybe that's Luke telling you they're coming home early," said Franny hopefully.

"No. It's Dewey," said Alice. "He says Zeb just figured out for sure what killed Damon."

"Really? Was it a drug, like he thought?" asked Franny.

"Yep. Something called diazepam," said Alice, squinting at her phone. "Oh—he says it's the same thing as valium."

"Valium? Isn't that a pretty common drug?" asked Owen.

"Apparently, it can be deadly given in a high dose when it's mixed with alcohol."

"Uh-oh," said Owen. "Does this mean someone mixed up a deadly cocktail and served it to Damon?"

"I don't know," said Alice, feeling sick at the thought that Taya's 'complimentary drink' might've had a bit too much of a kick to it.

"Valium isn't that hard to come by, is it?" asked Franny. "What if Taya *accidentally* killed Damon? Maybe she was just trying to teach him a lesson and didn't know he would react that way."

"That would explain why she turned fifty shades of pale when Alice told her what killed the guy," said Owen.

Alice's phone dinged again. "Dewey says he talked to Art Ross, over at the Bauble Box."

The Bauble Box was Blue Valley's one and only jewelry shop, and Art Ross was a full-fledged jeweler.

"Dewey asked him how someone could have removed the little stones from the Scarlett Lady, and Art said not just anyone could do that with a necklace of that quality. It would take a person with specialized tools who knows a thing or two about gem settings."

"I like that Dewey," said Owen. "Ben and Luke never want to tell us anything about their investigations. We always have to pry information out of them. But Dewey's an open book."

"I think Dewey's giving away as little as he can," said Alice. "With Ben and Luke away, he needs our help."

"We keep looking at this thing as a murder," said Owen, "but, it's really a robbery *and* a murder. If Damon went into the museum through the open window, then ran out the front door—and the only thing on him was the Grand Ole Gal—that means someone *else* came in first and painstakingly removed those little red stones, one by one."

"Leaving the big diamond behind," added Alice. "Wait a minute! What if Damon walked in on the thief just as he finished picking apart the necklace? Maybe Dewey swiped the big diamond simply because that was all that was left."

"But if he was smart enough to go in through the window, why be so sloppy and trip the alarm on his way out?" asked Franny.

"Because he was drugged!" said Owen. "He wouldn't have been making great decisions at that point—and that also explains why Pearl Ann said he was stumbling along, mumbling and acting so strangely. His system was full of both alcohol *and* drugs! Hold on a second. I just remembered something." Owen whipped out his phone. "Let's revisit some of the crimes from the other towns the faire has been to." He scrolled and read, nodding to himself. "Yep. Just as I thought. Most of the thefts in the other towns were jewelry, too. That, plus a few small paintings I've never heard of. A vase. Some collectible coins. Small items taken from small museums, mostly. Nothing with any world-class security. And there's another common thread. Get this: *Security Guard Found Asleep on the Job.*" Owen pointed at the headline from an article in a neighboring city. "Or how about this: *Guards Wake to Find Gems Missing.*"

"So . . . No one was ever killed. But it sounds like they were drugged," said Alice, feeling her heart begin to pound.

"Maybe that's the thief's MO," said Owen. "He or she knocks out whatever security is present, then makes off with the treasure."

"Remind me why we think the thief didn't take the Grand Ole Gal," said Franny.

"We still don't know why," said Alice. "But this does point to the idea that someone connected with the Nottingham Medieval Faire is both the thief and the killer."

In unison, three pairs of eyes looked across the lake to Cozy Bear Camp and Glamp.

"Pretty much everyone on the staff is staying right over there," Owen said.

"And they'll all be at the clearing for at least another few hours," said Franny.

"Someone should really go over there and do some snooping," said Owen.

Alice turned to Franny. "Franny, how are your feet?"

CHAPTER 11

They decided to ride their bikes around the back of the lake to avoid passing by the clearing where the faire was still in full swing. Lake Trail was an asphalt road that circled the entire lake, running past houses, weaving through trees, and along the water. The back side of the lake was less developed than the front, but cozy cottages were scattered here and there, and there were numerous trailheads for hiking from the lake to the mountains, as well as a lovely little park at the edge of the Cozy Bear Camp and Glamp property.

In years past, the place had been known simply as Cozy Bear Campground—owned and managed by Harve Anderson. It featured primitive camp sites, a smattering of charcoal barbecue grills, and a community bathroom with lukewarm showers. Harve considered this last feature to be something of an unnecessary luxury, but realized he needed to cater to campers who were less into roughing it than Harve himself was.

But that was before he fell in love with Sue, who brought to the table an appreciation for the finer things and an impeccable sense of style. Nowadays, visitors to Cozy Bear could pitch their tents or check into a luxurious yurt-like accommodation, complete with comfortable beds and electricity. Customers could enjoy hiking the trails up into the Smokies by day, and come home for a hot shower, a hearty meal, and lively entertainment by night. The barbecue pits were upgraded, and charcoal could be purchased in the camp store, along with scented candles, fine chocolates, and Cozy Bear Cub t-shirts. The trail heads were clearly marked and the trails inviting and well-kept. As a result, the place stayed pretty well booked year-round, and all kinds of "campers" looked forward to their visits to Blue Valley. All said, Harve loved Sue's influence in spite of himself, and he adored Sue even more.

As they approached the campground, Alice, Owen, and Franny got off their bikes and walked.

"So, we're looking for tools used by jewelers," said Owen.

"And valium," said Franny.

"Right," said Alice, as they approached the Cozy Bear's arched entryway, which was looking festive even in the dark, covered with lights and climbing roses that were putting on early blooms with the arrival of spring. When the three passed the little check-in building—a stacked-log affair that resembled a tiny cabin—Harve popped his head out.

"I was wondering if you three would show up," he said with a conspiratorial grin.

"We don't know what you're talking about," said Owen, giving Harve a wink.

"There's been a robbery and a murder in Blue Valley. That means you're making the rounds, asking the questions. It was only a matter of time until you got to us," said Harve with a laugh.

Franny, who was looking at the board where Cozy Bear's daily activities were always posted, read aloud: "*Moonlit canoe rides across the lake to the faire.* How cool is that?"

"Well, we do have quite a few guests who are in town for the faire," said Harve. "Course, we're mostly booked up with the faire people themselves. It's pretty entertaining, to tell you the truth. Sue and I can't step outside without seeing someone juggling or tumbling or telling fortunes. These people are a hoot! We had karaoke last night, and the whole group showed up. With all those talented show-offs, you can imagine how amazing that was."

"Indeed, we can," said Owen. "So, Harve, what time was karaoke?"

"It was supposed to run from seven-thirty to eight-thirty, but with all those hams competing for the mike, it went on until nine-thirty, I'd say."

"Can you remember who was there? I mean, were *all* the faire people there?"

"Almost all of them," said Harve.

"I can tell you exactly who was there," said Sue, who'd just come out of the check-in cabin. "I was in charge of giving out the awards—you know, silly awards, like Kookiest Dance Moves, and Most Fabulous Outfit. Anyway, I passed around a sign-up

MURDER STEALS THE SHOW

sheet." She handed a clipboard to Alice. "We've got thirty guests staying here from the faire."

"And twenty-nine of them were here for karaoke," said Alice.

"That's funny. I thought I counted twenty-seven," said Sue, frowning at the list. "I know that because I passed this sign-up sheet around at the beginning of the event and numbered them all for our door prize."

"Who's not on the list?" mumbled Owen, scanning the page.

"I don't see Wamba," said Franny.

"Nor is there a Ralph," said Owen. "What was Wamba's real last name, again?"

"Woods," said Alice. "Nope, Wamba's definitely not on this list."

"Is he the jester guy?" asked Harve. "No, he wasn't here for karaoke. A whole big group of them had gone into town, to the Smiling Hound. Most of them came back in time for karaoke. But not the jester."

"Wamba was the only one who wasn't here when the crimes were being committed," Alice said, still scanning the list. "Harve and Sue, could we take a very quick peek at Wamba's tent? Just to see if we need to call Officer Dewey to come out with a warrant?"

"Well, if you just *happened* to be walking by the tent at Campsite 8 and *accidentally* peeked in, I think that'd be okay," said Harve with a wink.

"I still can't figure out how I counted wrong," mumbled Sue, taking the clipboard back.

Alice, Owen, and Franny thanked the Andersons and walked over to Wamba's tent, which could probably be categorized as something between "glamp" and "camp." It was roomy, lit by a couple of battery-powered lanterns. Inside were juggling paraphernalia, props, costumes, and wooden scepters like the one Wamba had pulled out of his pocket earlier.

"This is eerie," Owen whispered, picking up the scepter with the smiling jester's head on top.

"Look at this," said Alice, who had just picked up a blanket that was wadded up on the floor, revealing a toolbox underneath.

Owen reached down and opened the lid. "Ah-ha! Needle-nose pliers!"

"I bet you could remove precious stones from a necklace with those," said Franny.

"There are some other really unusual tools in here," said Owen, digging around in the toolbox. "Wire cutters. A tiny, tiny file. The smallest drill bit I've ever seen."

"Why would a jester—or an accountant for that matter—need those?" asked Alice.

Suddenly, they heard footsteps approaching and someone said, "Hey!"

Alice, Owen, and Franny spun around, and were relieved to see that it was only Harve and Sue, standing at the entrance to Wamba's tent.

"We figured out why Sue's count was off at the karaoke," said Harve.

"These last two came late," said Sue, handing the karaoke list back to Alice, who held it to the lantern light.

"The Clarks," whispered Alice. Then she looked up at Harve and Sue. "Can we see their tent, as well?"

"Of course," said Harve. "We can stroll over that way together."

Lois and Drake had opted for Cozy Bear's finest accommodation—a glamping tent right on the water. The interior boasted wood flooring, cheerful lamps, and twin beds covered in plush comforters.

"Nice digs," said Owen, taking in the space. "I approve."

"Those dress forms are kind of creeping me out," said Franny, nodding at the two forms standing along the wall opposite the beds.

"That one is clearly supposed to be a male," said Owen, pointing at the more masculine form. "Do you still call it a *dress* form?"

"Who knows," said Alice.

"I'd be afraid of waking up and thinking one of them was an intruder lurking in the shadows," said Franny with a shiver.

"We should definitely bypass *Attack of the Killer Dress Forms* for movie night tonight," said Owen, patting Franny on the shoulder.

"What's this?" Alice opened a plastic case that looked like a tackle box. "Never mind. It's just a colossal sewing kit." She marveled at the accordion trays and tiny drawers and compartments, all filled with buttons, beads, needles, and tools. "I don't sew, so I don't know what any of this is for, but—"

"Someone's coming!" Harve, who'd been standing guard, whispered. "Hurry!"

Alice closed the sewing kit and they all scuttled out and moved far back into the shadows. As it turned out, the "someone" was only Javier, the friendly burro who lived on the grounds and enjoyed browsing the campsites for snacks when no one was around.

"Oh. It's Javier. Whew!" said Harve.

"Doesn't he sleep in a pen at night?" asked Alice, her heart still pounding.

"Yep. But he's an escape artist. That burro is a wild one."

All eyes turned back to Javier, who was by then standing near the tempting grass at the water's edge, and appeared to have nodded off mid-chew.

By that time, Alice, Owen, and Franny were all well

and truly spooked, and decided not to tempt fate any further. The faire across the lake was beginning to show signs of wrapping up for the day, and the first Cozy Bear campers were already paddling across the lake from Town Dock in their lantern-lit canoes.

"We'd better be going," said Alice, turning to Harve and Sue. "If you notice anything suspicious, let us know or call Dewey."

"You know we will," said Harve, with a little salute.

Goodbyes and thanks were exchanged, and Alice, Owen, and Franny pedaled back around the lake to the house. They had just parked their bikes and gone inside when Alice's phone rang.

"It's Luke," she said, bending to pat Finn, who was hopping about, wagging his tail.

"I'm pretty sure that's dog-speak for 'I need a potty break,'" said Owen.

"I'd better take this call—and this dog—outside," said Alice.

A few minutes later, she returned.

"What'd Luke have to say?" asked Franny, who had

removed her shoes and propped her feet up on the coffee table.

"He said a crew is working through the night, and the road will be clear tomorrow. He also said that he and Ben are doing everything they can to help Dewey from Runesville, and that we should leave it to them. I could hear Ben yelling in the background, telling us to stay out of the investigation."

"But Dewey needs us," said Owen.

"Ben's just worried about me," said Franny.

Alice's phone dinged. "And there's Dewey," she said.

"Read!" Owen ordered.

"He says he's been doing some research on Damon Huxley. It took a lot of digging, but he finally tracked him down." Alice's eyes widened as she scrolled through the message. "He'd changed his name! He used to be Todd Damon, and he's not from a wealthy family at all!"

"So how did he—" Franny started to say.

"Insider trading, apparently," said Alice. "He actually did time for it. It gets even better . . . or, worse, really.

Luke has a contact within the black market in Nashville."

"Ooh, how exciting!" said Owen.

"The contact apparently told Luke he was expecting something big to come down the pike from this area. A very rare, multi-stoned necklace worth around twenty-five million dollars."

"It has to be the Scarlett Lady!" said Franny.

"The black-market contact wasn't willing to tell Luke who his Blue Valley connection was, but when he found out Damon was dead—and thus, didn't need protecting—he admitted it!"

"So, Damon *was* the thief!" said Franny.

"But he didn't steal the whole necklace, as he'd apparently intended to," said Owen.

"He certainly didn't plan on dying with the diamond in his pocket," said Alice.

"I keep feeling like we're running around in circles," said Franny, who had found the bag of kettle corn from earlier and was munching away.

Alice thought back to morning the day before, when

she'd seen Damon watching the museum. "Let's piece together a possible scenario."

"Good idea," said Owen.

"Damon planned to steal the necklace and sell it on the black market," said Alice. "That's why he was casing the museum yesterday morning."

"Ethel said he came into the museum yesterday, so he could've unlocked the window," said Franny.

"At the very least, he could've honed in on the exact location of the necklace and checked how secure it was," said Alice.

"Hold on," said Owen. "I don't think Damon unlocked the window."

"Why?" asked Franny.

"Because if Damon had gotten there first, he would've stolen the whole necklace. Luke's black-market guy said he'd been told to expect multiple stones—a rare piece. Not just one giant diamond."

"Of course!" said Alice. "Since the door alarm hadn't been tripped, and the only other apparent point of entry was the window, the ruby thief must've gotten there first. Then, later, Damon got there and swiped what was left of the necklace."

"And then died," said Franny.

"What if Damon walked in on the original thief, and then that person drugged him?" Alice wondered.

"Just like at the other robberies!" said Owen. "With the sleeping security guards!"

"A strong enough dose of valium would definitely knock someone out," said Franny.

"And when that valium hit his system—" Alice started to say.

"Which was already full of alcohol . . ." added Owen.

"That would explain why Damon stumbled out the front door. He didn't care about setting off the alarm at that point. He knew he was in trouble. He stumbled into the alley and ran into Pearl Ann," said Alice.

"He was grumbling about the jester," said Franny.

Alice sighed. "Then, we came along, and I heard bells."

"What about Taya? And Mayor Abercrombie?" asked Owen, who had taken charge of the remote control and was searching for a movie to watch. "Are they still suspects?"

Everyone had gotten into their pajamas and was curled up on the couch, together with Poppy and Finn.

"The way Taya reacted when you told her about how Damon died was definitely strange," said Franny.

"Do we think that she served him a *cocktail of death*?" Owen said in his spooky voice.

"Then there's the mayor," said Alice. "As much as I hate it, we have to consider the fact that Damon was murdered the very same day that the scathing editorial was published in the newspaper—*and* that the mayor was at the scene of the crime."

"We have photographic evidence of that," said Franny with a shiver.

"I really don't see Mayor Abercrombie or Taya as jewel thieves," said Owen.

"Neither do I," said Alice. "I just hope they're not murderers."

CHAPTER 12

"We'd better hurry up and get over to the clearing," Alice said, putting down her empty mug early the next morning. "The whole crew will be there getting ready for the day, and it'll be the perfect time to feel out Wamba and the Clarks."

"We have a good excuse to be there, too, since we have to turn in our costumes," said Owen, putting the last pieces of his costume—his pointy ears—into the packing box they'd come in. "I'm going to miss these most of all," he said with a regretful sigh.

"Well, the bright side is, your ears are sort of naturally pointy," said Franny cheerily.

"They are?" Owen rushed over to the mirror that hung next to the front door. "They are! Maybe I really am part elf!"

"Please," said Alice, rolling her eyes. "Let's get these costumes back to the Clarks." She paused and shook her head. "They've been so gracious. I hate to think they could be criminals."

"What about Wamba?" said Franny. "He's a really nice guy, too."

"I'd still be willing to bet there's a bad apple somewhere in that bunch," said Owen. "Ooh! Maybe they're all in cahoots and committed the crimes together!"

"I hadn't even thought about that," said Alice.

"We elves are more than just pretty faces, you know," said Owen. "We're also shockingly brilliant and insightful."

Alice raised a brow at Owen, then proceeded to stack the costume boxes into his arms, one on top of the other. "Let's get going, smarty-pants."

"Then, we need to get over to Main Street," said

Owen from behind the boxes. "I have to bake twelve dozen chocolate scones, another twelve dozen Welsh cakes, and whip up some clotted cream this morning."

"Yum," said Franny, putting a hand over her stomach, which was growling audibly. "The baby wants a scone."

"Your baby has very good taste," said Owen.

"We'll drop off these costumes, see if we can pick up any clues, then head to work," said Alice.

"But only until one o'clock," said Franny.

"What happens at one o'clock?" asked Owen.

"Lois told me that she and her brother will be performing at the park. We can have lunch and watch the show."

"I do love a good acrobatic display," said Owen. "But, I suspect you're looking for an excuse to eat yet another roasted turkey leg." He gave Franny a knowing look, and she replied with a little shrug.

When they arrived at the clearing, the sun was just rising, and most of the faire staff had walked over from Cozy Bear and were quietly at work, resetting the grounds for the evening's events. It was the night of the grand ball, and the jousting ring was being transformed into an enchanting fairytale dance floor.

Alice spotted the Clarks wrapping flowered garlands around a tree trunk. "Good morning!" she called, pushing her bike while awkwardly managing Owen's as well. Owen's arms were still stacked high with the costume boxes, and Franny was leading him along by the arm since he couldn't see a thing in front of him.

"Let me help!" Drake quickly said, running to Owen and taking some of his load. "Just set them down right here, Owen. We've got use of the faire golf cart this morning. We'll run these back over to our tent at the Cozy Bear as soon as we're done here."

"We're looking forward to your show this afternoon," said Franny.

"Glad you're coming!" said Lois. "As soon as we're done with this, we're doing a run-through of some of the tough stunts right here in the clearing. You should hang around and watch!"

"You're so sweet," said Owen. "But, we all have to

get to work." He turned to leave, gave Alice a wink, then turned back to the Clarks. "Oh, by the way, our friend Ethel, the director of the Heritage Museum?" He paused and put on a regretful expression. Alice held onto a straight face as she waited to see what Owen was up to. "She was so distraught after losing that beautiful necklace. Since you specialize in spectacular costumes—which really is an art form, by the way—we were wondering if it would be possible to make a replica of the Scarlet Lady. To give as a gift to Ethel." Owen looked at Alice and Franny, who nodded, pretending to know what Owen was talking about.

"Well, we do know a thing or two about costume jewelry," Lois said slowly. "We've seen some amazing replicas."

"We're all about creating convincing props," said Drake proudly. "We once worked on a project that called for a replica of the Henckel Von Donnersmarck Tiara. That was a lot of fun."

"The heckle-von-what?" asked Owen.

"It's this famous German tiara," said Lois.

"You saw the Scarlet Lady, right?" asked Owen. "Do you think it'd be too complicated to copy?"

Lois looked at her brother. "It is a very intricate necklace," she said.

"We read all about it in the paper," Drake added. "From the looks of it, the little red diamonds would be pretty easy to copy, based on what I know about faux gemstones. We work with those all the time—like the ones on your costumes."

"And the giant diamond in the middle?"

"A believable one would cost a bit, but I bet we could find one," said Lois.

"Do you think you could do it?" asked Owen.

"I think so," said Drake. "A thing like that, done right, wouldn't be cheap, though."

Owen glanced at his watch. "We've got to run," he apologized. "We'll discuss it and check back with you later."

The Clarks nodded, and everyone wished everyone else a good morning.

"That was an interesting conversation," said Franny.

"I just wanted to find out whether the Clarks have experience working with jewelry," whispered Owen. "I think it's safe to say they do."

"Plus, they seem to have an interest in jewels," said Alice. "Let's go poke at Wamba now, then update Dewey."

"There's Wamba now," said Franny, as they walked their bikes toward the edge of the clearing, where Wamba was busy untangling a string of twinkle lights.

Before they caught up with him, Dewey pulled up in his police cruiser, lights flashing.

"What's going on?" Alice wondered aloud.

They got nearer the cruiser and watched in startled silence as Dewey stepped out and hurried over to Wamba.

"Ralph Woods?" he asked.

"Yes, that's me," said Wamba.

"I'm going to have to ask you to come with me," Dewey said.

"Wow, Dewey sounds just like one of the television cops," whispered Owen.

"What's this about?" Wamba asked.

"I'm sorry, Mr. Woods, but I'm taking you in for questioning."

"But I've already answered your questions." Wamba was clearly resisting complying.

Finally, Dewey had no choice but to elaborate. "Some stolen jewels were found early this morning in your pocket."

"What pocket?" Wamba shoved his hands into his pockets.

"Your costume from yesterday. Apparently, when your costumes were laundered, a couple of stolen gems were found."

"But I didn't—"

"In addition to that, you were at the scene of a murder the night before last." He glimpsed Alice. "And, you were seen having an altercation with the deceased. Do you deny it?"

"With that Damon jerk?"

"Do you deny you had a confrontation with him, Mr. Woods?"

Wamba dropped the twinkle lights and stared at the ground. "No," he finally said, and walked silently to the cruiser, where Dewey opened the door and Wamba climbed in. The window was open, and through it, Wamba could be heard grumbling angrily, "I'd do it again, too. That jerk deserved what he got."

As he went around to get in behind the wheel, Dewey gave a nod to Alice, Owen, and Franny, and pulled out of the clearing. The rest of the faire staff stood quietly in shock for a moment, then went back to work, whispering among themselves.

Alice, Owen, and Franny pedaled into town.

"Look, there's Taya," Owen said as they turned onto Main Street and approached the Smiling Hound.

"Let's tell her about Wamba," said Alice. "I'd rather she heard it from us than through the grapevine."

They slowed and came to a stop near Taya, who was walking down the sidewalk, about to go into the pub.

"Hi, Taya," Alice said. "We, uh, just saw something at the clearing that you're probably going to want to know about."

"What?"

"Wamba—or Ralph—was taken to the police station."

"Why?" Taya swallowed hard.

"Dewey took him in for more questioning. It didn't sound good."

"I don't understand."

"Some of the stolen gems were found in his pocket," said Franny.

"Plus, he was at the scene of the murder," said Alice. "And, he admitted to having a run-in with Damon."

"*Of course* he had a run-in with Damon," said Taya, her face clouding over with a mix of sadness and rage. "That jerk wouldn't leave me alone. Wamba—Ralph, that is—was defending me."

"Maybe he hit him a little too hard or something," said Franny.

"No, he didn't," said Taya. "I saw the whole thing! It

happened at the Hound. I was coming down the back hallway, and Damon was still at the bar. He saw me, came into the hallway, blocked my path, and started grabbing at me. Ralph saw what was going on, stepped in, and gave Damon a good shove. He didn't bother me anymore after that. I even went back to work the bar. With Ralph there, I felt safe. Then, they all left . . . And then . . ." Her voice faded and a tear rolled down her cheek.

"Taya, what is it?" Alice asked, putting an arm around her and helping her to a nearby bench to sit down.

"Ralph told me what happened after they all left the Hound that night," Taya said, taking a tissue out of her bag and blowing her nose. "He followed Damon. Said he was going to confront him one more time—tell him never to bother me again. He was walking down the street, searching for Damon, when Damon came stumbling out of the museum. The alarm went off, and Ralph saw that Damon was completely drunk, the way he was weaving around. He walked up to him, gave him a little shove, and Damon fell immediately. He was getting back up, furious, calling Ralph names, but then Ralph heard someone coming from behind the building and ran away."

"That would be Pearl Ann," said Owen, nodding. "She of the deadly handbag."

"That explains why I heard bells jingling in the distance," said Alice. "Wamba must've run away just as we were walking to the alley with Pearl Ann."

"Wamba couldn't have killed Damon," said Owen, "because Damon was still alive when Pearl Ann found him—and that was *after* Wamba had shoved him."

"This explains why Damon was ranting about 'the jester,'" said Franny. "He'd just had a fight with one!"

"Taya, you'd better get over to the police station right away," said Alice. "I'm pretty sure Dewey thinks Wamba had something to do with both the robbery and the murder. Maybe you can help clear that up."

"Ralph is no killer," said Taya with a sob. "I know that for sure. Because I know *exactly* who killed Damon Huxley."

"Who?" asked Alice.

"*Me*," said Taya. "I put something into his drink. I was just so sick of his unwanted advances, and the way he tried to belittle me. I wanted to teach him a lesson. But, I had no idea he would have a bad reaction. I swear, I didn't know!" She got up from the bench. "I've got to get to the police station. I have to clear this up! Poor Ralph!"

CHAPTER 13

The weather was perfect for an outdoor medieval faire—a blue sky with a few puffy clouds scattered across it, the flowers in the huge planters that lined Main Street in full bloom, and visitors and locals alike, walking around town, popping into shops and restaurants, and enjoying the shows and medieval food stands in the park.

"Main Street is hopping!" said Owen, leaning over the façade on the top of their building. "I just pulled the last batch of scones from the oven downstairs, and Hilda's in charge of the bakery for the rest of the day. I'm ready to put on my centaur costume and get down there!"

"I'm glad it's shaping up to be a nice day, after the

strange morning we had," said Alice, who was moving around the rooftop garden, watering plants.

"I know," agreed Franny, taking a seat to rest after trimming a few of the climbing vines that had gotten a little out of hand. "Now, we can finally relax and enjoy the rest of the faire. Ben and Luke are on their way home. Tonight's the ball. The day's going to be so much fun."

"Plus, it would seem the mystery of the Scarlet Lady is solved," added Owen. "Wamba—and also Damon—stole the jewels. And Taya—well, drugging Damon was the wrong thing to do, but I know she never meant to truly hurt him. Hopefully, the judge will believe that."

"So the thief and the murderer didn't turn out to be the same person after all," said Alice. "They turned out to be *three* different people."

"What do Ben and Luke think about all this?" asked Owen.

"I texted Luke right away when Taya confessed to drugging Damon," said Alice. Her phone buzzed. "I bet that's him now," she said, pulling it out of her pocket. "Uh-oh." Alice put down her watering can and held her phone with both hands, reading through the message.

"Uh-oh?" Owen went and looked over Alice's shoulder.

"Taya put a *laxative* into Damon's drink," said Alice.

"That old trick!" said Owen, which got him looks from both Alice and Franny.

"So . . . not a mega dose of valium?" asked Franny, who had jumped up and was reading over Alice's other shoulder.

"Nope. And there's more. They found the valium had been given by injection," said Alice. "Not by mouth."

"Did Wamba kill Damon after all, then?" asked Franny. "Is Wamba the person who's been committing all of the thefts in the wake of the faire—and this time, he leveled up to murder?"

These questions were met with a long pause.

"I wonder if Ethel ever remembered which faire staff members came into the museum before the robbery, other than Little John and Gabby," said Alice.

"She said it was two men and a woman, right?" asked Franny.

"I think so," said Alice.

"I'll text her," said Owen, pulling out his phone.

Before they'd even had time to ponder the matter any further, Owen's phone dinged.

"She remembered!" he said triumphantly. "The old steel trap worked!"

"What did Ethel say? Who came into the museum?" Alice reached for Owen's phone, but he quickly swiped it away.

"Drumroll, please," he said with a sly smile. "Ethel says she saw the three at the faire last night and specifically checked their names. She looked around for us, but of course, we'd left early."

"Sorry about that," said Franny.

"Don't be. Your poor swollen feet couldn't help it," said Owen, and he held up his phone with Ethel's message displayed on the screen. "Wamba. Drake. Lois."

"But didn't the Clarks say they hadn't been to the

museum?" asked Alice. "That they'd only read about the necklace in the newspaper?"

"That's how I remember it," said Franny. "Why lie about that?"

"If the old steel trap is working properly, the Clarks, along with Wamba, *did* come into the museum, so any one of them could've unlocked that window."

"We've already confirmed they weren't at the campground when the crimes took place," said Franny. "Maybe Owen's idea was right. Maybe more than one person committed the crime, and Wamba wasn't working alone."

"It doesn't sit well that the Clarks lied about having been at the museum. As far as I'm concerned, they just moved to the top of the list of suspects," said Alice.

CHAPTER 14

"So, your butt is inflatable?" asked Franny, patting the horse's backside that bounced along behind Owen as they walked down Main Street toward Town Park.

"Yep. There's a little fan in there," said Owen, who wore a brown leather-like vest, and an impressive mane of gleaming brown hair, and carried a bow and arrows. "I just keep my two front legs moving, and the rest of me follows!"

"Cool!" said Franny.

"And *you*," said Owen, "look like some kind of mysterious, beautiful woodland creature." Franny's costume for the day featured flowers set around small horns that protruded from her brown hair, and a leafy green knee-length gown with blue flowers scattered over it.

"Thank you!" Franny looked down at her skirt. "I made it myself."

Franny and Owen looked at Alice.

"Your costume is, um, very nice," Owen said slowly.

"Yes! Very nice," agreed Franny. "What are you . . . supposed to be?"

"Franny! How could you not know?" asked Alice. "I'm a giant turkey leg!"

Light dawned simultaneously in Franny and Owen's eyes, which was followed by a few minutes of uncontrollable laughter.

"Get a grip," said Alice, rolling her eyes. Her turkey drumstick costume was a little bit itchy, and a little bit hard to move around in, if she was being honest. It was one giant, brown, pear-shaped piece, with four holes for Alice's arms and legs, and another for her face, which peeked out through the opening just beneath the 'bone' part of the drumstick.

"You're definitely going to be in the running at the

Fairest of the Faire contest this afternoon," said Owen, wiping a tear from his eye.

"Shut up," said Alice, hiking her bag up onto her shoulder and trying to pick up her pace, but found it challenging since she could only very quickly move her legs from the knees down.

"You're a turkey drumstick carrying a messenger bag," said Owen. "What do you keep in there? Napkins?"

This was followed by another round of giggles from both Owen and Franny.

Alice looked over at the Heritage Museum as they passed it on the way to the park, and her steps slowed. She walked over and looked into the front window, at the display of photos from faires past. Next to them was a poster about the Scarlet Lady exhibit, with the word 'Cancelled' pasted across it.

As she read the words beneath the photo of the necklace, something on the edge of Alice's memory bothered her. She set her bag down on the bench outside the museum, opened it, and took out the newspaper from two days earlier with the front-page article about the necklace.

"Ethel clearly didn't make this poster," said Alice, pointing.

"Definitely not," said Owen. "That poster probably comes with the exhibit. It's a professional job, for sure."

"It's beautiful," added Franny. "They must put these in the windows wherever the necklace is on display."

"Read the description of the Scarlet Lady," said Alice.

Owen squinted at the words. "An Old-World treasure is visiting your town! The world-famous Scarlet Lady was given to Spanish explorers in Tennessee by Queen Isabella of Spain—and now you can see it for yourself! Marvel at the twenty-three-carat diamond at the center of the setting, affectionately known across the state as the Grand Ole Gal. Then, feast your eyes on the tiny red diamonds around it, amounting to a total of nearly seventy carats! These extremely rare gems, together with the Grand Ole Gal, make the Scarlet Lady worth over twenty-five million dollars!" Owen took a deep breath. "*What?*"

By this time, Alice had found the part of the article in the newspaper that she'd been looking for. "Ah-ha!" she said. "I *knew* something was off!"

"What is it?" asked Franny, leaning over to read the words.

"The article in the *Blue Valley Post* is an interview with Ethel. Ethel mistakenly called those red stones rubies. Not diamonds."

Owen had already whipped out his phone. "It says here that red diamonds are the rarest and most valuable of all!"

"We've been thinking the Grand Ole Gal was the big treasure," said Alice. "But the little stones around it are worth far more."

"This is amazing!" said Franny.

"Something else has been bothering me, but I couldn't quite put my finger on what it was until now," said Alice.

"That you're too fatty and greasy?" asked Owen.

Alice gave Owen her evil eye. "That the Clarks have called them diamonds all along," she said. "They knew more about that necklace than anyone else in town. We were all going by what Ethel said. But the Clarks knew better."

Alice shoved the paper back into her bag and slung it over her shoulder as best she could. The three of them walked on toward the park. When they got there, they saw Little John and Gabby standing near the gazebo, and were surprised to find that they were talking to Wamba.

"Oh, I'm glad to see you three," said Little John in his booming voice as they approached. "Wamba's just come from the police station."

"We saw you leaving the clearing this morning," Alice said to Wamba. "Dewey didn't arrest you after all?"

"Nope," said Wamba. "The little red stones in my pocket were from Little Wamba's hat." He pulled the marotte from his pocket and jingled it at Alice. "The jeweler examined them and said they were just very well-made fakes—like the ones on my hat." He pointed at his sparkling hat, its three points jingling when he moved his head.

"Also like the ones on my gown," said Alice. She thought of the gorgeous gown, of the sparkling stones scattered across the bodice—many of them red . . . And of the last-minute alterations the Clarks had insisted upon, the same day as the robbery, even though Alice knew the dress fit perfectly.

"Wamba. Ralph. I have a question for you," said Alice.

Wamba looked Alice right in the eye and nodded.

"Why do you have a bunch of specialized tools in your tent?"

"Because of my hobby," said Wamba, pulling his pocket watch from his pocket and flipping open the case. "I collect old pocket watches. Didn't I tell you that?" He paused for a beat. "Wait, how do you know about my tools?"

Alice didn't take the time to answer this. "Little John, where are the Clarks?" she asked.

Little John frowned at the urgency in Alice's voice. "They'll be here in about an hour," he said.

"Their performance was supposed to be at one o'clock," said Franny, looking at her watch. "It's five 'til."

"They postponed," said Gabby, pointing toward the gazebo, where the Gothic Trolls had drawn quite a crowd, and the sweet sounds of a dulcimer, harp, and lute floated through the air.

"Ooh—they're playing my favorite. *The Epic Adventure of Lyle, the Hircocervus*," said Owen, applauding.

"Alice, what's going on?" asked Little John.

"Is that golf cart available?" Alice asked, waddling at top speed over to a Nottingham Faire golf cart that was parked nearby.

"Yes," said Little John, taking out the keys.

"To the Cozy Bear, right?" said Wamba. "I'm coming with you!" He leapt into the back of the cart.

"So am I," said Little John, taking the wheel.

"Me, too," said Gabby, squeezing in beside Little John.

They all piled into the cart, which groaned under their collective weight as they pulled away from the curb and Little John turned to drive back down Main Street toward the lake. More than a few heads turned to see the golf cart looking more like a clown car, stuffed with medieval characters—a giant turkey leg and the tail end of a centaur hanging over the back.

"Now will someone tell me what's happening?" Little John asked as they sped along.

"The Clarks are making a run for it," said Alice. "Owen, call Dewey!"

CHAPTER 15

As she ran toward the Clarks' glamping tent, Alice was reminded once more how difficult it was to run in a turkey leg costume. She stumbled several times and actually fell down once, tearing her brown tights and skinning her knee.

"You're waddling," said Owen with a snicker, as he and Franny helped Alice up.

"I can't help it!" said Alice, dusting herself off as best she could and glaring at Owen. "Do you think I *planned* to run in this getup?"

When they arrived at the Clarks' yurt, the first things to greet them were the two dress forms, now wearing Alice and Owen's costumes. They had been carefully picked over, so that certain gems were missing, with threads hanging down from the empty spaces left behind. In several places, the fabric had even been torn, as though the Clarks had been in a hurry to harvest the jewels.

"I've been at the gate all day," said Harve, peering into the yurt. "The Clarks came in about an hour ago, but they never left or checked out or anything. They must still be here somewhere."

"We need to split up," said Alice. "Little John—you, Gabby, and Wamba check the other tents and the campground. Harve and Sue, guard the gate and watch for Dewey. Owen, Franny, and I will head into the woods and check the trails. I know a back way out of the campground. Maybe they went that way."

Everyone dispersed at top speed, and Alice finally began to catch her stride in her costume. She, Owen, and Franny moved among the trails and rustic campsites tucked back into the woods, but there was no sign of the Clarks—only a few campers who were surprised, to say the least, at the sight of a giant turkey leg, centaur, and woodland nymph running through the woods. Alice was just beginning to get discouraged when she saw something shiny, glinting in the sun to the side of the trail.

"Wait!" she said. "What's that?"

On closer inspection, they found a snippet of holographic fringe.

"I remember this!" said Franny, examining the find. "Several of the performers have this fringe on their costumes!"

"We're on the right track, then," said Owen, looking further down the trail they were on. "Let's keep going."

Just as they started to move further into the woods, which were rapidly closing in around them, Alice heard a twig snap.

"Wait—did you hear that?" she whispered, her heart pounding.

"What?" asked Owen. "Oh—I can hear a distant siren. Dewey's on the way!"

Then Alice saw it. "Look!" She pointed toward a large clump of bushes. "You can come out now, Lois and Drake," she called, feeling more confident as the police siren got nearer.

"We know you took the jewels. You might as well give it up," said Owen.

There was a bit more movement in the bushes, then Lois and Drake emerged, looking defeated.

"How did you figure it out?" Lois asked quietly, stepping in front of her brother.

"We put the clues together. You knew the little red stones were diamonds when everyone else thought they were rubies. You lied about having been to the museum Wednesday. You weren't here at the campground when the robbery was taking place," said Alice. "It all added up."

Lois glanced over her shoulder at Drake. "I guess we'd better turn ourselves in," she said, taking another step closer to Alice.

"I guess you're right," Drake said.

Alice tried to see him around his sister. He was holding something in his hand. Some kind of rope. Suddenly, in one swift movement, Drake swung one end of the rope at a limb overhead. The rope wrapped around and caught on the limb.

"It's a bola wrap!" Owen yelled as Drake deftly climbed the rope and in a blur, began swinging. As he swung over Lois, she grabbed his legs, and at the highest point, flipped in the air, landing on her feet on the other side of Alice, Owen, and Franny. She lunged at Alice and before Alice knew what was happening, her arms were pinned behind her, and Drake had landed on the ground next to her and had whipped out a loaded syringe.

"No one was supposed to die, you know," said Lois, tightening what felt like a cord of some kind around Alice's wrists. "No one's ever died before."

"I'm sure you'll be fine, Alice," Drake added, taking the cap off the needle and squirting a tiny bit of fluid through it.

When Owen made a move toward Alice, Drake put the needle near her shoulder, which was covered only by a thin layer of brown fabric.

"Get back!" Lois threatened.

Drake turned his head at the sound of the police car,

which had clearly arrived at the campground. "Here's what's going to happen," he said calmly. "You're going to let us leave, or else Alice here is going to be taking a very long nap."

"Apparently, this stuff sometimes kills people, so you probably don't want to risk it," said Lois.

Owen and Franny immediately gave them some space. Alice felt tears stinging her eyes.

"That's better," said Drake. "You two go and have a seat by that tree, and Lois will tie you up."

Owen and Franny did as they were told, and within seconds, they were secured to the tree with the bola wrap.

"Good work," said Lois. "We'll be on our way now." She looked at Alice. "By the way, Alice, that's the dumbest costume ever."

Even in her precarious position, Alice felt a little insulted.

Suddenly, Dewey could be heard calling from the main campground. "Owen! Alice! Franny!" he yelled. "Where are you?"

Everyone froze.

"Not one sound," said Drake, holding the syringe an inch from Alice's arm.

As Dewey's voice began to grow a bit more distant, Alice realized he'd taken the wrong trail. She took a deep breath and made a decision.

"Dewey! We're here!" she yelled at the top of her lungs, surprising everyone.

"Bad choice, turkey leg!" said Drake.

Just as he was about to plunge the needle into Alice's arm, a wooden juggling ball flew through the air and hit him squarely in the head. He gave a yelp of pain, stumbled, and fell backward onto the ground, dropping the syringe.

Then Alice kicked Lois in the shin—a move she was able to make even in her restrictive drumstick costume. "That's for calling my costume dumb!"

Wamba joined Alice, whacking Lois and then Drake in turn with Little Wamba, all the while, Owen and Franny cheered from their tree. Within seconds, Dewey, Little John, and Gabby found them—and moments later, the Clarks were being led away in handcuffs.

"And that, my friends, is how it's done," said Owen, dusting his hands.

Alice linked arms with him and Franny, and they walked together down the trail, back toward the campground and the lake.

"Ben's going to go nuts when he hears about this," said Franny, laying a protective hand over her belly. She sniffled quietly. "I think it's just now hitting me that we were in real danger there for a minute."

They stopped walking, and Owen pulled both women in for a group hug.

"We're safe. It's all over," he said.

"How are you feeling?" Alice asked, wiping a tear from Franny's cheek.

Franny smiled. "Your costume is making me hungry."

CHAPTER 16

The sun was just beginning to get low in the sky over Blue Lake when Ben and Luke finally rolled into the drive.

Alice, Owen, and Franny were relaxing on the dock, drinking mugs of tea with a platter of turkey legs on the table, along with cheeses, chocolates, Scotch eggs, and a crusty loaf of bread they'd bought at the faire.

Finn's ears perked up and his tail wagged furiously as car doors could be heard slamming shut on the other side of the house. Even Poppy, who'd been lounging lazily in the grass, stood and stretched.

Franny flew to Ben's side as he walked down the hill from the house.

"You're finally home!" she said.

"Finally," said Ben, smiling at his wife and giving her a kiss.

Luke walked over and took Alice's hand and pulled her out of her seat and into his arms.

"I missed you," he said into her ear.

Alice looked into his eyes, took in the beard stubble and messy hair, and thought him more handsome than ever. "I missed you, too."

"This is quite a feast," said Ben, looking over the spread.

"I thought you'd all be at the faire when we got home," said Luke.

"We thought we would be, too," said Owen. "But somehow, after the last few days, it sounded more appealing to sit out here, watch the sunset, and stuff ourselves."

"I couldn't agree more," said Ben. "I love the faire, but we're exhausted."

"And hungry," added Luke, looking at the goodies on the table.

"Besides, the faire will be going on until Sunday afternoon," said Alice. "We've still got two more days to enjoy it." Ben and Luke happily filled their plates and took their seats on the dock.

"So, tell us about the part of the day when you were all tied up and a criminal was holding a hypodermic needle to your arm," Luke said, raising a brow at Alice and taking a big bite of his turkey leg.

"Or the part of the day where you two were tied to a tree," Ben said, giving Franny and Owen a wry smile.

"You heard about that?" Franny asked.

"Dewey filled us in," said Ben, reaching for Franny's hand.

"Then you know we helped Dewey catch two jewel thieves," said Owen. "I figure we're in line to receive some kind of award for assisting the police."

"You do deserve an award," Luke said. "But I don't like the part where you were in danger." His eyes landed on Alice.

"That wasn't our favorite part, either," she said.

Just then, Little John and Gabby walked down the hill, still in full costume.

"Hello!" Little John bellowed. "Thought we'd walk over from the clearing to thank you again for your help. You broke the curse!"

"You're heroes," added Gabby. "The Clarks have confessed to every single one of the robberies in the towns we've visited—including a clinic, where they got the valium."

"And the murder?" Alice asked.

"That, too," said Gabby. "But, it sounds like it truly was an accident. They'd done the routine many times. The high dose of valium would put the security guard to sleep. Then, they'd swipe the jewels or whatever they were stealing, and by the time the guard woke up, they'd be long gone."

"They didn't count on Damon showing up drunk," said Little John.

"That's right," said Luke. "It seems that Damon had planned to steal the Scarlet Lady himself. But when he passed the museum on his way home from the

Smiling Hound that night, he caught sight of the Clarks inside, and the open window, too."

"He went in through the window, angry that someone had beat him to the punch," said Ben.

"Since there was no security guard to deal with at the Heritage Museum, the Clarks had hatched a slightly new scheme," Luke said. "They planned to remove the red diamonds from the necklace and replace them with fakes like the ones they used in the props for the faire. Then, they'd return the necklace to its case in the museum, in the hopes that the robbery would go unnoticed for at least a few days. But when Damon confronted them and grabbed the Grand Ole Gal, they did what they always did: gave him a shot of valium to settle him down. Unfortunately, he reacted badly, ran out the door, and died."

"When he set off the alarm, the Clarks escaped out the same window they'd come in through," said Ben.

"Wow," said Owen. "If Damon hadn't gone after the necklace, the Scarlet Lady would still be in the museum, but with fake gems, and who knows when anyone would've noticed it."

"Exactly true," said Little John. "One more good

thing has come of this as well. Our own Wamba is in love!"

"With Taya?" asked Franny.

"Yep. They're planning to keep in touch when the faire moves on. No idea what the future holds, but let's just say Blue Valley may gain an accountant, who can juggle, one day in the future."

"Wamba suspected the Clarks all along but was afraid to say anything, since he had no proof," said Gabby.

"That explains the riddled clues he gave us," said Alice. "He told us right from the beginning that if we found the jewels, we'd find the killer."

"Sharp as a tack, that Ralph," said Little John. He turned to Gabby and took her hand. "Well, my lady, I guess we'd better return to the faire. We'll see you all tomorrow."

As the two walked up the hill and through the trees toward the clearing, they passed Dewey, who was heading toward Ben and Franny's.

"Dewey, I don't think I've ever seen you out of uniform," said Franny, motioning for Dewey to sit in the empty chair next to Owen. "You look very handsome."

Dewey looked down and blushed a little. "I'm here to thank you for your help these past few days. And to welcome you two home," he said to Ben and Luke. "And to make a small request."

"Sure," said Ben. "What is it, Dewey?"

"Please never go up into the mountains again."

Everyone laughed and enjoyed a wonderful dinner. The music from the ball could be heard in the distance, mixed with the peaceful lapping of the water and chirping of the crickets. The sun had almost slipped behind the mountains, and the water had turned a lovely mix of pink and lavender when Owen stood up.

"Let's take an after-dinner walk," he said. "Good for the digestion."

"Good idea," said Luke. "I'll go up and get Finn's leash."

A few minutes later, they were walking along the winding trail that ran between Ben and Luke's houses. Once they reached Luke's cabin, they started to turn and head back to Franny and Ben's, but Owen stopped them.

"Let's walk a little further," he suggested.

"Good idea," said Alice. "It's so nice out."

The whole group meandered past Luke's cabin along the trail around the edge of the lake a bit further.

"Stop," said Owen suddenly.

"Why?" asked Alice, looking around.

They were standing next to an old stone cottage, its little porch overlooking the water, its ends both capped with chimneys. It was set in a semicircle of flowering dogwood, and though the place clearly needed work, there was something enchanting about it in the fading light.

"Owen, what is this place?" asked Alice.

"Isn't this the old Callahan cottage?" asked Ben.

"It is," said Owen. "Or, it used to be. Now it's the James cottage."

"Owen, what's this about?" asked Alice.

"I wanted you, my best friends—my family—to be

the first to see my new house. Or, my old house, depending on how you look at it."

"Owen! You bought this place?" said Alice, feeling a wave of happiness bubbling up in her chest. "It's charming!"

"You've talked about getting a house on the lake for forever!" said Franny. "Now, we're going to be neighbors!"

Owen was patted on the back, congratulated, and hugged for some minutes after that. They all toured the cottage and Alice could see that it held great potential, and that Owen's sense of style would bring it back to life beautifully.

There was even a little stone path that led down to a dock from which both Ben's and Luke's houses could be seen.

"We'll be able to send each other messages with our flashlights at night," said Franny, taking Owen's arm.

"Ooh, we'll have to devise a secret code," said Owen.

As they began the walk back to Ben and Franny's, Luke took Alice's hand and they walked along in comfortable silence for a while.

"I'm so happy for Owen," Alice finally said. "I can't wait to see what he does with the place."

"How great is it that we'll all be out here at the lake together?" Luke said.

Alice took a few more steps, then stopped.

"What?" asked Luke, turning to face her.

"So that's how you imagine the future? All of us, out here together?"

Luke caught her up in his arms and kissed her until she felt like she was melting.

"Yes, Alice Maguire," he said softly. "I see us all here, as neighbors. I see children running back and forth between our houses. I see dinners on the lake and coffee on the rooftop. But when I think of my future, the only thing that really matters . . . is that you're in it."

Alice felt a great wave of something between joy and peace washing over her.

And then Luke was down on one knee.

"I was going to ask you on New Year's Eve. I was going to ask you at the faire—at the ball. I was going to ask you like a thousand different times, but I wanted to wait for the right moment." He smiled. "And I think this is it. Alice, I want to marry you. I want to share . . ." He thought for a moment. "I want to share *life* with you."

He kissed her hand, and Alice felt tears stinging her eyes.

"Will you marry me?"

Up ahead, Alice saw her friends. In the distance, she could see the lights of the faire glowing merrily from the clearing. She knew already that the night would hold a snuggle on the couch and a movie at Franny and Ben's. The next day, they'd all go to the faire together. The next summer, there would be a new baby in the family—this family they were building. Wonderful things—unthinkably wonderful things— were in store.

"Yes!" Alice said.

Luke jumped up and swept her off her feet—literally. Then he set her back down, kissed her warmly, and they began walking again.

"I don't have the ring here," Luke apologized with a

chuckle. "Didn't know this was going to finally be the right moment."

They both laughed and Alice smiled up at the sky. Overhead, a million stars twinkled.

"Making a wish?" Luke asked, noticing Alice's gaze.

Alice laughed, knowing that she already had everything she could ever want, right here.

She smiled and shook her head slowly. "Nope."

AUTHOR'S NOTE

I'd love to hear your thoughts on my books, the storylines, and anything else that you'd like to comment on—reader feedback is very important to me. My contact information, along with some other helpful links, is listed on the next page. If you'd like to be on my list of "folks to contact" with updates, release and sales notifications, etc.… just shoot me an email and let me know. Thanks for reading!

Also…

… if you're looking for more great reads, Summer Prescott Books publishes several popular series by outstanding Cozy Mystery authors.

CONTACT SUMMER PRESCOTT BOOKS PUBLISHING

Twitter: @summerprescott1

Bookbub: https://www.bookbub.com/authors/summer-prescott

Blog and Book Catalog: http://summerprescottbooks.com

Email: summer.prescott.cozies@gmail.com

YouTube: https://www.youtube.com/channel/UCngKNUkDdWuQ5k7-Vkfrp6A

And…be sure to check out the Summer Prescott Cozy Mysteries fan page and Summer Prescott Books Publishing Page on Facebook – let's be friends!

CONTACT SUMMER PRESCOTT BOOKS PUBLISHING

To download a free book, and sign up for our fun and exciting newsletter, which will give you opportunities to win prizes and swag, enter contests, and be the first to know about New Releases, click here: http://summerprescottbooks.com